'I'm not going to listen to what you have to say. I don't want to hear it any more. Leave me alone.'

'It wasn't like that, Sarah,' said Matthew. 'I don't want to see you upset like this. I want to help you, if only you will let me. If I could just make you understand...'

He drew her to him. 'Let me show you...'

His lips came down on hers, gentle at first, exploring the softness of her mouth as though he would soothe all her troubles away. She was too startled to resist, too taken up in the powerful surge of her emotions to even think of pulling away. Then he moved in closer and deepened the kiss, and she lost the will to fight him.

'Sarah,' he murmured, 'you have to believe me... I want you to be happy. I want to take away all the hurt and unhappiness. Let me help you.'

'No, I can't.'

When **Joanna Neil** discovered Mills & Boon®, her life-long addiction to reading crystallised into an exciting new career writing Medical Romance™. Her characters are probably the outcome of her varied lifestyle, which includes working as a clerk, typist, nurse and infant teacher. She enjoys dressmaking and cooking at her Leicestershire home. Her family includes a husband, son and daughter, an exuberant yellow Labrador and two slightly crazed cockatiels. She currently works with a team of tutors at her local education centre to provide creative writing workshops for people interested in exploring their own writing ambitions.

Recent titles by the same author:

THE DOCTOR'S FAMILY SECRET
A CONSULTANT'S SPECIAL CARE
EMERGENCY AT VALLEY HOSPITAL
HER CONSULTANT BOSS

CHALLENGING DR CARLISLE

BY
JOANNA NEIL

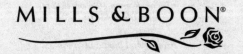

First published in Great Britain 2004
Harlequin Mills & Boon Limited,
Eton House, 18-24 Paradise Road, Richmond, Surrey TW9 1SR

© Joanna Neil 2004

ISBN 0 263 83906 0

Set in Times Roman 10½ on 12½ pt.
03-0604-45470

Printed and bound in Spain
by Litografia Rosés, S.A., Barcelona

CHAPTER ONE

GLANCING at her watch, Sarah hurried towards the conference room, her breath snagging painfully in her lungs. She had already missed the first talk that had been scheduled for the morning, and she was late, more than half an hour late, for this second event of the day. That wasn't good by any standards and it didn't matter a jot that it wasn't her fault, did it?

Doctors were meant to be on time—it showed professionalism, commitment and dedication to duty. Sarah was fairly sure that she had all of those qualities, but who would believe her? Certainly none of the doctors who had made sure that they were here for the start of the meeting.

She pulled open the door of the conference room a fraction and peered inside.

'So, I hope we can all agree that every second counts,' the speaker was saying. His voice was deep and compelling, satisfyingly smooth on the senses. 'Now, if you will, I want you to try to imagine the scene.'

Sarah frowned. There was also something vaguely familiar about that calm, confident tone, but she quickly dismissed the notion as fanciful thinking. Her nerves were in a state after the rush to get here, and she was pretty sure that her reasoning wasn't to be trusted right now.

'Let's suppose that there has been a major incident in the city centre,' the speaker went on, 'and there are casualties suffering from multiple injuries, along with burns or perhaps the effects of chemical inhalation. Can we be sure that we, as doctors, will be prepared to deal with every eventuality?'

Sarah pulled the door open wider and tried to creep into the room without being noticed, but the manoeuvre was doomed to failure from the outset. The door gave a loud creak of complaint, and at that moment it seemed as though everyone in the room had turned to see who it was who had dared to interrupt the proceedings. She froze.

'Well, possibly not,' the speaker said in an amused drawl, half turning and throwing a glance in her direction. 'Especially if there are those of us who leave it to the last minute to turn up.' His audience laughed.

Aware that everyone was staring at her, Sarah felt her cheeks burn. She looked down at the floor, wishing that she could disappear into a black void, but it wasn't to be. Her hair fell in a golden cloud of curls around her face and she hoped it might serve to hide the evidence of her embarrassment from the watchful eyes of the assembled throng.

'I'm so sorry,' she managed, feeling incredibly foolish and not wanting to risk looking up at him directly. 'I must apologise for being late. It was unavoidable, I'm afraid.'

She glanced around, searching desperately for a

seat that she could slink into at the end of an aisle. There wasn't one, though, and she scanned the rows of chairs in the hope of finding an empty place close to hand.

'There's a spare seat here at the front. Come and make yourself comfortable.'

Sarah was rooted to the spot for a second or two. There it was again…that distinct note of familiarity about the voice. She stared up at the man, a feeling of unease growing in her. From where she stood he was partly in shadow, but when she flicked back her hair to get a better look, she could see that he was tall, lean and fit-looking, and that he was wearing an expensively tailored grey suit, the jacket worn loose to reveal a fresh linen shirt and stylishly subtle tie. Then he turned fully towards her, and for the first time she saw him properly, face on.

She drew in a shocked breath. Matthew—was it really Matthew? Her mind began to reel. It must have been all of four years since she had last seen him, and now here he was, as large as life, standing there looking as energetic and forceful as ever. His hair was still as black as night, cut in those customary crisp, attractive lines to frame the angular face that she knew so well.

His eyes narrowed on her as recognition dawned on him, too, but he simply said, 'Why don't you come and sit down? As soon as you're settled we can get on.'

It was a mild reproof and it brought her to her

senses so that she quickly moved to do as he suggested.

'Thank you,' Matthew murmured. He waited while she slid fluidly down into the seat and smoothed her pencil-slim skirt with a shaky hand. Then she crossed one long shapely leg over the other and tried to gather her composure.

Watching her, his brows met briefly in a dark line, then he turned to face his audience once more. 'Now, where were we? Ah, yes…the major incident in the city centre. I was alluding to the fact that every second counts, and I should thank the young lady for emphasising my point. Had we been involved in a life-threatening situation when she walked in, I expect that by now most of our patients would probably have passed away.' There was a ripple of good-humoured laughter from the audience, and Sarah felt a flush of heat run along her cheekbones all over again.

'Perhaps we should ensure that we have some sound strategies in place for the next time.' Matthew was soon in his stride once more. He was a convincing, authoritative speaker, and it was clear to see that he knew everything there was to know about emergency procedures.

The last few years must have cemented all his ambitions. He was still in his early thirties, and yet here he was, a consultant, a man that people looked up to for advice and expertise. It wasn't unexpected. It had always been on the cards that he would do well for himself. As long as she had known him, he had been a high flyer, and now, she acknowledged with a wry grimace, he had success written all over him.

The meeting broke up an hour or so later, and Sarah looked for a quick getaway. She didn't want to stop and meet up with him. Even after all the years that had gone by, her feelings were still ragged. Her sister was still hurting, and her family was struggling to recover in the aftermath of her father's misfortune. Things would never be the same again.

She headed for the door, but there were crowds blocking her way as people stopped to chat to one another, and she heard snatches of comments about Matthew's talk. It had gone down well, by all accounts, and now Matthew was surrounded by a huddle of doctors who wanted to talk to him.

She tried to gently push her way through the mass of people, but it was like wading through deep water and she was getting nowhere fast. In the background she heard Matthew saying urgently, 'Sarah…wait.'

She pretended not to hear, and she had almost reached the door when he appeared by her side. 'Sarah, don't go.'

His long fingers settled around her arm, and a quiver of nervous anticipation ran through her as she absorbed the warmth of his touch. His nearness had always had this effect on her. Nothing had changed.

'We should talk,' he said. 'It's been a long time.'

'Yes, it has.' She grimaced. 'I'm in a bit of a hurry, though. Anyway, you've already had a laugh at my expense today. I'm not sure that I want to hang around so that you can do it again.' There was a faint edge to her voice. 'Your talk went down very well, I thought. I'm glad I could help.'

He looked at her guardedly. 'You're not holding that against me, surely? That isn't like you. It was a light-hearted moment, nothing more, and it helped to ease the tension in the room. Don't you think you're taking this too seriously?'

She gave him a tight smile. 'Ah, but isn't that what I do? I seem to recall you saying something along those lines once before. I'm the quiet, thoughtful one, remember? I'm the girl who gets on with her studies and makes sure that everything runs to order. Rachel, now, she's a fun girl, and she's good to be with. Everyone wants to get to know my sister.'

It wasn't an exact imitation of what he'd said way back in the days when their two families had been on good terms, but it was near enough, and it would do.

He frowned, letting go of her arm. 'I said that, but I didn't mean it in the way you make it sound. You and your sister are two very different personalities, that's all. It doesn't imply that either one is any better than the other. Why did you never say anything at the time, if it bothered you?'

'It didn't bother me,' she said, lying through her teeth. 'I could see that you and Rachel were busy having fun, and that was fine by me. It was only what I expected once you and she started to share a flat.'

His mouth creased into a smile. 'That was a long time ago. We were young, and we were both of a mind to enjoy life back then. We didn't take anything too seriously, and you know Rachel…she was restless and she often wanted to go out and paint the town red. As to the flat, we weren't on our own. You make it sound as though there was just the two of us, but it wasn't like that. There were other people who shared it with us. It seemed like a practical thing to do at the time.'

'Yes, that's what I thought. I expect Rachel did, too, but all the same it came as a blow to her when you left. She was never very happy after that.'

A muscle flicked along the line of his jaw. 'I know she was upset around that time, but I had to go. You know I did. I had to start a new job, one that had been tailor-made for me. I was leaving to take up a post as a specialist registrar in one of the best units in the country. There was no way I was going to turn it down. It was something I'd always wanted.'

'I'm sure it was perfect for you…and now here you are, a consultant, no less. You have the world at your feet.'

He frowned, and she guessed that he was puzzled by the thread of irony in her tone. 'What about you?' he asked. 'How are you doing?'

His glance skimmed her slender figure, gliding over the stretchy cotton top and the skirt that lovingly moulded itself to her hips, so that she felt immediately self-conscious.

'You're certainly looking well.' He smiled, his mouth moving in that engaging way that had always had the effect of sending her weak at the knees. 'I heard that you'd qualified as a doctor. Your father must be very proud of you.'

Her mouth made a brief twist of acknowledgement. 'He's always supported me in whatever I've done.' She looked around, feeling uncomfortable now that the conversation had turned to her, and she noticed that some individuals were trying to get Matthew's attention. 'I think people want to talk to you,' she murmured. 'I won't take up any more of your time.'

He ignored her attempt to break away from him. 'Are you going to be here for the rest of the conference?'

'Yes. Well, for this evening's lectures anyway.'

'Will you be staying here in the hotel?'

She nodded. 'It's too far away from home for me to want to attempt the drive back late at night. I'll probably make an early start first thing in the morning.' She took a step away from him. 'Look, you'll have to excuse me, I have to go and make a phone call.'

She half turned, and a young man took the opportunity to grab Matthew's attention. 'Mr Bayford? May I have a word?' Sarah began to edge away.

Matthew ignored the man, keeping his gaze firmly fixed on Sarah. 'Maybe I'll see you later?' he suggested.

'Maybe.' And then again, maybe not, if I happen to see you first, her inner voice added.

This time she managed to get away without incident, and she headed straight for the lobby, aware that Matthew was once more surrounded by admirers. He would be kept occupied for some time, she guessed.

All at once, she felt the need for some fresh air.

She was worried in case Matthew tried to come after her, and perhaps it would be for the best if she walked some distance away from the hotel. There was a break of at least a couple of hours before the next lecture, and maybe she would have time to take a stroll along the seafront. Devon was a beautiful county and if she spent just a little while enjoying the scenery it would help her to gather her thoughts and give her a chance to put things into perspective. Meeting Matthew again after all this time had stirred up feelings in her that she had hoped had been buried long ago.

Besides, arriving so late at the conference meant that she hadn't been able to find a space on the hotel car park and she had been forced to leave her car some distance away along the seafront. It might be just as well to go and check that it was secure.

The sky was a clear blue, and the sun was warm and soothing on her bare arms as she walked. She followed the line of the shore, taking comfort in the tranquil landscape, and a few minutes later, in the shelter of a quiet cove, she used her mobile to phone home. Rachel answered within a moment or two, sounding relieved to hear Sarah's voice.

'You got there safely, then? I was worried that the business with Dad would have upset you.'

'I'm fine. I didn't want to leave him, but I thought if I stayed it would have made his condition worse. He seemed to be getting more and more agitated at the thought of me abandoning my plans. There's just no reasoning with him when he gets into that state, is there? How is he?'

'He seems to be much better now, but he had more or less recovered before you left. Whatever it was that you gave him seemed to do the trick, but I made him go to the hospital with me as you suggested. I've been worried about him for a long time now, and it seemed like the ideal opportunity to get him there.' She gave a faint sigh, and Sarah could imagine her shaking her head at her father's stubbornness.

'They checked him over and said that the ECG showed up some irregularities, but they said they didn't think that it was anything to cause immediate concern. They gave him an appointment to see a specialist in a few months' time, and said that he would need to have some tests. Does that mean that he's suffering from some kind of heart trouble?'

'I think the whole episode was more of a warning sign. Angina, probably, brought on by the stress of losing yet another client. I could see that he was knocked for six this morning when he received the letter. It doesn't seem fair. He works so hard and it all seems to be for nothing.'

'He's up against so much competition these days. Other companies are undercutting him all the time.'

'I think his customers will regret leaving him in the end. They won't get better medical equipment anywhere else. He's brilliant at design work and everything he provides is custom-made. Perhaps that's where he's going wrong. He makes things too well, to too high a specification.'

Sarah pressed her lips together. 'You will keep an eye on him, won't you, Rachel? I'll get back as soon as I can tomorrow, but I want you to be sure to ring me if there's any problem.'

'Of course I will. You don't need to worry. How are things at your end? Is the conference going all right? I'm glad you didn't abandon it. The attendance counts as part of your training, doesn't it?'

'Yes, but that doesn't matter. It's working out fine.' She wasn't going to tell Rachel that she had met up with Matthew. There was no point in distressing her unduly. Rachel had enough on her plate right now.

She finished the call a few minutes later and walked along the headland to explore the rest of the beach area. Beyond the cove, where she had parked her car, the seafront had been developed in order to cater for holidaymakers. There was a boating lake where children were clearly enjoying the water activities, and further along there were trampolines and go-karts.

Sarah stood and watched the children at play. Narrowing her eyes against the glare of the sun, she followed the antics of two boys as they manoeuvred their motorised inflatable boat between half a dozen others on the lake. In another boat, a girl and a boy who looked to be about eight years old were trying to bring their boat in to the side. The boy was guiding it along the concrete edge of the lake where there were stanchions to secure the ropes in place.

'The attendant's busy,' the boy said. 'You'll have to get out and tie the rope around the pillar. I'll try and keep it steady.'

The girl nodded and jumped up, rocking the boat.

She steadied herself and then made to step up onto the landing stage. All would have been well if it hadn't been for another couple of children trying to bring their boat alongside at the same time. The attendant looked over at them and must have sensed that things were going wrong because he hurried forward, ready to help.

He was too late, though. The two boats collided and the girl missed her footing and fell, cracking her head against the concrete.

Sarah was already running towards them. The attendant reached out to grab the child but missed, and Sarah could see that the girl was slipping under the water between the boat and the edge of the lake.

She didn't stop to think. She flung her bag down by the side of the lake and jumped in. Wading towards the girl, she could see that she was limp in the water, and there was blood trickling from a wound at her temple. 'It's all right,' she said quickly. 'I've got you.'

The boy was beside himself with anxiety. 'Will my sister be all right? It was an accident. I didn't mean it to happen.'

'I know that you didn't,' Sarah reassured him. 'I'll get her out of the water and look after her. What's her name?'

'Jessica. I'm Tom.'

'All right, Tom. You stay there and let the attendant help you out of the boat.'

White-faced, he did as she told him, and Sarah was thankful that the children in the second boat had stayed where they were. They looked too frightened to do anything, and she thought that she could safely leave them to the attendant. Right now, he was reaching out to help her with the girl.

'I'm a doctor,' she told him when they were safely back on dry land and she had gently laid the girl down on an area of grass nearby. 'You see to the other children. I'll stay with her and do what I can for her. Perhaps the boy can go and fetch their parents.'

He nodded. 'I feel terrible about this. I was watching some other children further along. It all happened so quickly. Usually there are two of us here, but my mate's gone to the hut to replace one of the oars for the rowboats. He should be back any minute.'

Sarah made a swift examination, and it was plain to see that the girl was in trouble. She had a nasty head injury and she was slipping in and out of consciousness. Sarah was worried about her condition. Reaching for her bag, she brought out her phone and dialled for an ambulance.

'Do you have any newspapers in the hut over there?' she asked the attendant when he came back to her a short time later. 'I need something that I can roll up to make a temporary neck brace in case there's a spinal injury. I could do with a roll of tape, too.'

'I'll go and have look and see what I can find,' he said.

He came back a moment later with a sheaf of papers. Sarah took them and began to roll them up, quickly fashioning a makeshift collar and carefully placing it around the girl's neck. She secured it in place with a length of tape.

'That should do the trick for the moment, but I need some medical equipment from my car,' she told him. She leaned back on her heels and eased her wet clothes away from where they were clinging to her damp skin. 'It's just a few yards away from here, in the parking bay…the blue car. You can see it from here. Do you think you could go and get the things I need? I don't want to leave the girl.'

He nodded. 'My mate's here now. He'll see to it that everything's under control with the boats. What is it that you need?'

'My medical bag and a white box. They're both in the boot.' She handed him her car keys and told him the registration number.

'I'll be as quick as I can,' he said, and hurried off.

Sarah checked the girl's responses once more. Things were not looking good, and she wished that she had more experience in emergency medicine, especially paediatrics. Matthew would have known instantly what to do. He would never have any doubts, she was certain, and for a wild moment or two she wished that he could be with her now. She shook her head, ridding herself of the thought. Was she mad? The last thing she needed was to have Matthew by her side. That would only stir up everything that had gone before.

'What happened?' A woman came and knelt beside Sarah, looking desperately worried. 'Tom told me there had been an accident. What's wrong with my daughter?'

'She banged her head. We need to get her to hospital as soon as possible. I'm a doctor, and I'll do what I can for her until the ambulance comes.'

As soon as the attendant came back and deposited the medical bag and the box on the floor by her side, Sarah set to work. She quickly set up an airway and asked the mother if she would operate the ventilation bag. 'All you have to do is press with your fingers, like this, and keep up a steady rhythm. Do you think you can manage that?'

'Yes, I'll try. Is this the right way to do it?'

'That's perfect.' Sarah guessed that the woman was glad to be able to do something.

She worked quickly to establish an intravenous line, and explained to the child's mother what she was doing. 'I'm going to take some blood, so that the hospital can cross-match it. It will speed up the process at the other end. I'm also giving her an analgesic to relieve the pain.' She was beginning to be concerned by the girl's deteriorating level of consciousness.

'Something's wrong, isn't it?' the mother said suddenly. 'Why is she jerking like that? Is she having a fit?' Her voice was rising with tension.

Sarah nodded and tried to reply in a calming tone. 'It does sometimes happen after a head injury. I'll give her medication to see if I can bring it under control.'

The woman's features were taut with strain as she

watched Sarah work. 'It's serious, though, isn't it?' She sounded tearful. 'What's going to happen to her? Will she be all right?'

'We won't know exactly what's going on until we can get her to the hospital and the doctors there can do tests. They will probably need to take X-rays and do a CAT scan. You can be reassured that they will do everything possible to minimise any damage.' She carefully checked the girl over once more. 'At least the fitting has stopped.'

An ambulance siren sounded, drawing nearer, and Sarah was relieved that it had arrived quickly. 'I'm sure that you and Tom will be able to go with her to the hospital. Try not to worry—she'll be in good hands.' She glanced at the boy, who was looking increasingly distraught. 'Maybe you need to do what you can to reassure Tom. He's very upset about what happened, but it wasn't his fault.'

When the paramedics approached, Sarah quietly reported events to them. 'We need to contact a neuro-surgeon as soon as possible.'

The paramedics nodded. 'We'll do that. You can leave her with us. We'll take good care of her.'

'Thanks.' Sarah watched as they gently lifted the girl onto a trolley and settled her into the ambulance.

'Thank you for doing what you could to help,' the mother said shakily. 'I'm so grateful to you for looking after her.'

'I'm just glad that I was around when it happened. You take care.'

Sarah waited, watching as the ambulance moved

away. Then she collected her bag and her keys, along with her medical equipment, and made her way to her car. She stowed her medical bag and the box safely in the boot, then set off once more for the hotel.

She was even more conscious now that she was dripping wet after her immersion in the water, and she needed to think about going back to the hotel and getting changed into dry clothes. She just hoped that nobody would see her going up to her room. She had made an exhibition of herself once already today, and she had no desire for it to happen again.

In fact, she managed to slip into the hotel through a back entrance, and a helpful young woman receptionist offered to send up a pot of coffee to her room to warm her through.

'I'll send room service up with it right away. You go and get yourself out of those wet things.'

'Thanks.' Sarah didn't need telling twice. She took the lift to the second floor and let herself into her room. Maybe she would be able to rinse her clothes through in the bathroom and hang them out to dry on the balcony. She didn't want to wait for room service to launder her clothes. It might take too long for them to get them back to her, and she wanted to be ready to leave early in the morning.

Sarah unlocked the glass doors that opened out onto the balcony. They were sticking a little and she struggled with them for a while, but at last she managed to get them open. There was a cooling breeze and a glorious view over the wide sweep of the bay, but Sarah was in too much of a hurry to take it in just now. Looking around, she saw that there was a wrought-iron railing that she could use to hang out her skirt.

'Room service.' There was a knock at the far door and a young woman entered the bedroom and slid a tray down onto a low table. A fierce draught of air shot through the room and out on to the balcony, and Sarah guessed that there must be an open window somewhere that had caused the through-flow. To her dismay, the glass doors slammed shut. The maid glanced up to see where the noise had come from, but then decided it was of no account and let herself out again.

Sarah tried the door and found that it was stuck fast. Now what was she to do? She rattled the handle and pushed with all her might, but it wouldn't budge. 'That's all I need,' she muttered, 'to be stuck out here for the rest of the day.' She started to bang on the door as hard as she could.

'Is something wrong? Can I do anything to help?' Out of the blue, Matthew's voice came from the neighbouring balcony.

Sarah stopped banging and swivelled round to face him. 'What are you doing there?'

'This is my room. I was just getting ready for the next lecture when I heard an unholy racket coming from out here.' He looked her over, his blue eyes widening. 'What on earth happened to you? You look like a bedraggled sea nymph.'

She pressed her lips together. She already knew

that she must look a mess. 'I've been in the boating lake. It's a long story.'

His mouth made a faint twist. 'I'm intrigued. I think I'd like to hear it.'

'I dare say you would,' she said tautly, 'but I'm afraid I have other things on my mind just now. I need to get back into my room, but the door seems to be stuck.'

'Let me have a look at it. I'll see if I can open it for you.' With one easy motion, he swung himself over the wrought-iron rail that separated the two balconies. His legs were long, and as he moved she could see the way the fabric of his trousers stretched taut against his muscled thighs. A ripple of heat ran through her.

He tested the door. 'Yes, it's certainly stuck.' He pulled the handle down and pushed hard, and infuriatingly it gave way at his first attempt. 'There you are.' He inspected the woodwork. 'It seems to have warped a little. That's probably why it jammed. Maybe you should have a word with the management in case it happens again.'

'Thank you,' she murmured, still put out by the ease with which he had managed it. 'I guess I need to grow some muscles.'

He gave her an amused smile, his glance drifting down over her so that she became uncomfortably conscious of the way her wet clothes clung to her body. 'I don't think so,' he said drily. 'I doubt they would suit you.' He leaned against the door, his arms folded negligently across his chest, his long body relaxed.

She desperately wanted to get back into her room, but it was impossible while he was blocking her escape route. 'I need to go and get changed,' she muttered. 'If you'll excuse me?'

'Of course. In exchange for you telling me what happened.'

She grimaced. 'There was an accident. A little girl banged her head down at the lake and had to go to hospital. I was near at hand so I was able to help out.'

Matthew frowned. 'How is she?'

'It's too soon to say. I'm going to phone up later and find out. In the meantime, I'm soaked and I have to sort out a spare set of clothes. I'm just thankful I have my overnight bag with me.'

His mouth tilted at the corners. 'It just isn't your day, is it? First you turn up half a day late, looking flustered and out of sorts, and now here you are with every appearance of a drowned sprite.'

Her green eyes flashed. 'I suppose you must be finding all this really amusing.'

He eased himself back against the doorjamb. 'You have to admit, this is not the Sarah that I knew. You were always so sensible, so in control of yourself. This is a Sarah who is completely new to me, and I confess I'm intrigued.'

'I can't imagine why. I know that a lot of time has gone by, but perhaps you're confused because the truth is, you never really knew me.'

She wished he wouldn't stand there, blocking her way, so sure of himself, so disturbingly male that her senses were going frantic. It was disconcerting, to say the least. She had thought she was over all that, but now all the feelings that she had thought she had laid to rest were clamouring for attention once more.

'Do you think so?' He appeared to be considering that. 'You could be right, I suppose. I think I shall look forward to discovering the new you.'

She shook her head. 'That's not likely to happen, is it? You and I will be going our separate ways once the conference is over.'

'That's a possibility, of course, but it doesn't have to be that way.'

She thought about that for a moment, disturbed by the prospect of seeing him again, but he pulled open the door and motioned her into the room with a wave of his hand, so that she had no time to dwell on it.

Sarah was all too aware that he had followed her inside. He glanced around. 'Looks as though room service have provided coffee, along with two cups. That's handy. Shall I pour?'

She could see that she wasn't easily going to get rid of him. 'If you like. I'll go and get into something dry.' Perhaps, if she took her time, he would lose interest and go away.

It wasn't to be. He was still there when she came back into the room a few minutes later, but she was feeling better after a quick shower, and more at ease now that she was dressed in a smoothly fitting shift dress.

He sent her an approving glance. 'Suits you,' he murmured.

'Better than the wrinkled wet look anyway.'

'Oh, I don't know about that.' He gave a half-smile. 'The wet look does have its advantages.'

She sent him a narrowed look, but he deflected her, saying thoughtfully, 'Is that one of Rachel's creations that you're wearing? She always did have a flair for what was stylish.'

'Clever of you to notice.' She walked over to the table and picked up her cup, sipping slowly, savouring the rich flavour of the coffee. 'Yes, it's one of hers.'

'Is she still working in fashion design? I wondered if she was still with the same company?'

'No. These days she works for herself.'

He raised a brow. 'That's interesting.'

It was more a question of necessity, but she wasn't going to tell him that. Since Rachel had given birth to Emily, just under nine months after Matthew had left, her options had been few and far between. As a single mother she struggled to keep the balance between bringing up her child and earning a living.

'What are you doing these days?' he asked.

'I'm in my last year of training. I'm starting a six-month stint as a senior house officer in Accident and Emergency on Monday.'

'Oh? Where is that? Is it local?'

She nodded. 'I'm going to work at the hospital near where I live. I was lucky to get the position. It means that I can stay close to my father and keep an eye on him.'

'How is he? Have things improved for him?'

'If you mean, is he still in business, then the answer

is yes. He's a survivor. He's had to be, but it's taken a toll on him. He's not well these days. That's why I was late arriving here today.'

'I'm sorry to hear that.' Just then his mobile phone rang, and he frowned and reached into his pocket to retrieve it. Answering the call, he listened for a moment or two, then looked up and said to Sarah, 'I'll have to go and deal with this. I'll see you later, I hope.'

She didn't answer him, but watched as he went out into the corridor and let himself into his own room.

She shut the door behind him. It had been disturbing to meet up with him again after all this time. She hadn't been prepared for the way he made her feel. All those confused and conflicting emotions that she'd kept locked inside her since he'd gone away four years ago had returned in full force, but they wouldn't do her any good. There had never been any point in loving Matthew. He had never returned her feelings.

It was just as well that she was leaving this place tomorrow. She would put distance between them once more and try to get on with her life.

CHAPTER TWO

'EMILY, sweetheart,' Sarah said gently, 'do you think you could come and put your dolly in her pram? I need to clear the table so that I can get the tea ready for Mummy and Grandad.'

'But me haven't changed her nappy yet,' Emily objected. She picked up a doll's dress from a pile on the table and examined it carefully. 'And her clothes is messy.'

Sarah cast an affectionate glance over her niece. She was a pretty child, just over three years old, with blonde curls and wide blue eyes, just like her mother. 'Are those the dresses that Mummy made for her?'

Emily nodded, her bright curls dancing with the movement. 'This one's the bestest.'

'They're all beautiful, aren't they? Your mummy's very clever.' She helped Emily move her doll and all the belongings that went along with her into the dining room, just off the kitchen.

'Me going to be dress 'signer when me grown-up,' Emily announced importantly.

Sarah smiled at her. Emily didn't have a care in the world. If only life could be like that for the rest of the family.

As it was, Rachel had gone to lie down a couple of hours ago, complaining of a bad headache, and when her father had come home from his day at the workshop, Sarah had noticed that he looked weary and fraught.

He came into the kitchen now, sniffing the air. 'Something smells good in here…what is it? Shepherd's pie?'

Sarah nodded. 'That's right. I know it's one of your favourites.'

He smiled. 'You make it the way your mother used to. Just the right blend of everything.' He sent her a thoughtful glance. 'It's good of you to come and help out like this. I sometimes think we put on you too much. It bothers me that we call on you so often.'

'You know I'm happy to do what I can,' Sarah commented mildly, looking up at him while she set out cutlery on the table. His hair was showing streaks of grey, emphasising the paleness of his features, and there were lines etched on his face that were evidence of the difficult times he had been through. 'Things haven't been easy for you lately, have they? Has the business been giving you more trouble?'

'No more than usual. I'm just about managing to keep on top of things.' He grimaced. 'Actually, it's Rachel that I'm worried about. She's not been herself for a long time now. Well, if the truth be known, she hasn't been the same since Emily was born. I've always thought it was the shock of becoming a single mother that brought about the change in her. Before that she was always happy-go-lucky and carefree and, although I've always tried to be supportive, I think it has been difficult for her to come to terms with the

way things are. She's found it hard to cope sometimes, but I do know that she's glad of your help.'

'We're a family and it's only right that we should
help each other out,' Sarah said quietly. 'As a matter
of fact, I've been worried about both of you these last
few weeks.'

'You've enough to think about with starting your
new job,' her father said. 'You work such long hours,
and I know that when you go to work in Accident
and Emergency you're going to find it stressful. It
can't be easy, battling to save lives every day.'

'I expect it will be rewarding, though,' Sarah said
with a smile. 'I'm a little nervous about making a start
but, from what I hear, old Mr Sheldon is a good man
to work for. He has a lot of experience behind him,
and I think I'll learn a lot from being on his team.'
It had been a while since this new posting had been
arranged, but at last the time had come around and
she was due to begin her stint as senior house officer
tomorrow.

She took the shepherd's pie from the oven and began to serve out the meal. 'I wonder if Rachel is feeling up to eating with us?'

'Go up and have a word with her, if you like. I'll
see to the rest of this and keep an eye on Emily.'

'OK. You just need to put the vegetable dishes out
on the table.'

Rachel stirred as Sarah walked into the room. 'How
are you feeling?' Sarah asked. 'Has the headache
cleared up at all?'

Rachel tried a smile. 'It's a bit better, thanks. The migraine tablet seems to be working.'

'Do you think you could manage anything to eat?'

'No, I don't think so, not yet.'

'Not to worry. I'll put it on one side for you to have later.' Sarah looked at her sister with concern. 'You've been getting these migraines quite a lot just lately, haven't you? Do you have any idea what's bringing them on?'

'I can't think of anything.' Rachel frowned. 'But you're right. They are getting worse.'

'Is there something on your mind? You know, stress can sometimes start these things off, and if there's something troubling you, perhaps it would help you to talk about it.'

Rachel gave a grimace. 'I shouldn't be stressed about anything, should I? I have a beautiful little girl, and Dad has let me come home so that I have a roof over my head. I don't know how I would have managed if he hadn't said that I could stay here, but it must make life difficult for him, because I'm not able to contribute much.'

'I don't think he sees it that way. You keep house for him and you prepare the meals. I'm sure he's grateful to you for that and he doesn't expect you to do any more.'

'It doesn't seem to be enough, though.' Rachel pulled a face. 'I feel so guilty. I know that the business is taking a downturn again and I feel that I must be a drain on him. I should be independent, and able to take care of myself without imposing on him.'

'You mustn't think like that. He's glad to have you here, I know he is, and I know that Emily is glad to have her grandad around.'

Rachel winced. 'Let's face it, he's the only father figure that she has. I've let her down. She's started to ask me why she hasn't got a daddy like her friends.'

That was awkward, Sarah could see that, but it was probably bound to happen sooner or later. 'Have you ever thought about getting in touch with her father?' she said softly. 'You've kept all this to yourself for such a long time, and you've done your best to try to manage on your own, but I could never understand why you wouldn't say who he is.'

'It would cause too many problems if I did that. I don't want to create trouble where there's no need.'

Sarah frowned. Unwillingly, her thoughts swung back to the day of the conference, and a vision of Matthew filled her head. Was he Emily's father? It hurt to dwell on the possibility, but it had to be faced. Rachel had had plenty of admirers in the past, but Sarah had never known her to show an interest in anyone but Matthew. He had been the one man who had spent a great deal of time with her, and they had seemed to share a special bond.

'Perhaps if you involved Emily's father in her up-bringing, it would make you feel better.'

'I won't do that. I can't. He has to get on with his own life, and we aren't ever going to be a part of it.'

'Does it have to be that way? Surely you could get in touch with him and talk things through? Even after all this time it shouldn't be too late.'

'No. It's not possible.' Rachel was adamant. 'It would never work out and it would be too hurtful all round. Besides, he's building up his career. He doesn't need a woman to slow him down. I'm just going to have to get through this the best way I can.'

Sarah could see that Rachel was beginning to get upset, and she thought better of probing any further. 'All right. If that's how you want it, I won't interfere. But if you should change your mind, if ever you want talk about it, I'm here for you. You know that, don't you?'

'Yes, I know.' Rachel tried a smile. 'Thanks, Sarah. I know that you mean well. I'll be all right, just as soon as I get rid of this headache.'

Sarah looked at her in sympathy. 'I'll leave you to rest, then. Try to get some sleep and you'll probably feel a lot better when you wake. I'll take care of Emily and see to it that she gets to bed on time.'

She kept her promise, and saw Emily settled before she left. Emily would be safe with her grandad to look after her, and if there were any problems he would give Sarah a ring.

'Don't worry yourself, Sarah,' her father said. 'They'll be fine with me. Go on home and try to get a good night's sleep, because you need to be fresh for your new job tomorrow.'

Sarah took his advice, and made sure that she was up bright and early next day. She was determined to make an early start in the A and E department, and more than anything she wanted to make a good impression.

'Ah, there you are.' A senior nurse inspected Sarah's name badge and greeted her with a smile. 'So you're Dr Carlisle. It's good to meet you. I'm Helen, the triage nurse. I'm glad that you're here in plenty of time. We've been rushed off our feet already this morning. There was an accident on the bypass in the early hours, and we've only just finished dealing with all the casualties.'

'I'm sorry to hear that. I hope everyone came through it all right.'

'We didn't lose anyone, if that's what you mean, but that's probably down to our new consultant. He seems to be very much on top of things, which is a relief. It can be difficult working with someone you don't know, but he took everything in his stride.'

'New consultant?' Sarah queried. 'I thought Mr Sheldon was in charge.'

'Oh, you obviously haven't heard the news. He was involved in a car smash a couple of months ago, and suffered a compound fracture to his leg. It was such a shock, and we were devastated when he decided to take early retirement on health grounds. We were all sad to see him go. He was such a good man.' She gave a brief smile. 'Now we're getting used to having Mr Bayford in his place. He's a much younger man, but he certainly knows what he's about.'

'Mr Bayford?' Sarah felt the colour drain from her face. 'Matthew Bayford?'

'That's right.' Helen looked at her curiously. 'Do you know him?'

Sarah nodded. 'I do. That is to say, I haven't

worked with him, but I've known him for a long time. We used to live in the same neighbourhood.'

'Oh, you'll be off to a flying start, then,' Helen said with a smile.

Sarah wasn't at all sure about that. She was still reeling from the shock of learning that he was in charge, but there was no time to dwell on it because all at once the paramedics arrived with a patient in cardiac arrest and everyone raced into action.

Sarah didn't see Matthew anywhere around, but she guessed that he had either gone off duty for a spell or he was dealing with another patient. She was simply relieved that he wasn't there right then. She needed time to get used to the idea that he was going to be around.

It was just under an hour later that she met up with him. 'We've a little boy coming in,' he said briskly to Helen. 'Luke Simpson. Four years old…suspected poisoning from iron tablets that were prescribed for his mother. We're not sure how many he's swallowed, but we'd better be prepared for the worst. Children think these things are sweets and swallow them by the handful sometimes.'

He looked up and saw Sarah. 'Hello.' He sent her a wry smile. 'I thought you and I would meet up this morning. This is your first day in A and E, isn't it? Is everything going all right so far?'

'It has been, up to now,' she said. He could take that how he pleased.

His eyes narrowed on her. If he had caught her sarcasm, he chose to ignore it. 'You'll soon get used to it. It can be a bit scary at times, but we're here to help. If you're not sure about anything, don't be afraid to ask.'

'I won't.'

'Did you find out how the little girl at the boating lake was doing?'

She nodded. 'I rang the hospital, and they said that she was on the mend.'

'That's good news,' he murmured. 'It was lucky for her that you happened to be around at the time.'

Helen moved away to prepare for the incoming child. Matthew waited until she had gone, and then said, 'I looked for you at the hotel, but the receptionist told me that you had left before breakfast.' His mouth made a crooked shape. 'You weren't trying to avoid me, by any chance, were you?'

'Why would I do that?' she countered, with an attempt at bravado. Even so, she couldn't hide the slight flush of heat that ran along her cheekbones. 'As to expecting to see me this morning, you certainly kept quiet about that, didn't you? You could have told me that you were working here. As it is, I only found out when I came in this morning.'

'Is that going to be a problem?' He gave her a thoughtful look. 'You and I go back a long way, but for some reason things seemed to have soured between us. We always used to be good friends, and I'm not sure that I know why things have changed.'

She made a faintly wry face at that. 'Friends, yes,' she murmured. In fact, hadn't he always treated her like a kid sister, as someone who had always been there in the background to be teased and sometimes humoured? It hadn't exactly been what she had wanted.

For herself, she had loved him, secretly and unreservedly, but always from a distance, afraid to reveal her true feelings, because she had been afraid that he would find her lacklustre next to her dazzling, fun-loving sister.

'What went wrong?' he asked. 'You've been cool towards me ever since we met up again at the conference. Does this have something to do with Rachel or the business with your father?'

'Do you really need to ask?' She sent him an incredulous look, her green eyes widening. 'When my dad's partner emptied the business bank account of money and disappeared abroad, it affected all of us. Rachel found it especially hard to deal with the aftermath, and all the more so because your parents had invested in the business and took their frustration out on us. She was beside herself with worry. Dad almost lost the house and she didn't know what she could do to help him. You were supposed to be her friend, but suddenly you weren't there for her any more. You let her down.'

'I'm sorry, but I don't see it that way at all. She knew why I had to go. It wasn't as though it was unexpected—it was something I had planned for some time, and I did what I could to help her through all the trouble. I did my best to smooth things over with my parents as well, but they were angry and upset, and all the more so because things had got into the local newspaper.'

He frowned. 'Anyway, if we're getting down to basics, why was Rachel the one who needed support? She wasn't the one who suffered the most in all this. Your father was. He bore the brunt of it and, as I recall, between you and Rachel, you were the one who would have been hurt the most by what happened.'

He searched her face. 'You were living in the house with your father at the time, and you were closer to what was going on, but I didn't hear you complain. Perhaps you were more upset about what happened than you let on at the time, but I don't remember you going to pieces over any of it. As I recall, you drew out the bulk of your own savings to help your father out of the mess he was in. Didn't you use the money that your mother and your grandparents left you?'

'It was what they would have wanted. Rachel would have done the same, if she had been able.'

'Now, that was never going to happen, was it?' he said with dry cynicism. 'If Rachel ever had any money, she spent it. She's always believed in living for the here and now.'

'So you blame her for that? Is that what happened? You didn't feel the same about her any more?'

Matthew's mouth twisted. 'No, it isn't like that at all. Give me credit for having a little more integrity than that. Rachel and I always got on well together and we understood very well what made each other tick. She isn't perfect, and neither am I. As to the rest of it, she was upset about what happened with your father, but she knew all along that I would be leaving at some time or another. It was just unfortunate that everything came together at the same time.'

Sarah glared at him, tight-mouthed. She wasn't in any way convinced by his argument, but there was no time to take it further right then because the doors of the department were pushed open as paramedics wheeled in the little boy they were expecting.

He looked very poorly, Sarah thought. He had been vomiting, and was doubled up from intestinal cramping.

'He's probably lost a lot of blood with the diarrhoea,' Matthew said, becoming professional in an instant. 'The poor little chap looks in a bad way. Let's get blood tests to check serum iron, along with full blood count, glucose and arterial blood gases. He's drowsy, and he's been convulsing. I'm worried that he'll go into shock. We need to act quickly.'

'Are you going to do a stomach washout?' Sarah asked.

'Yes. We have no choice if he's to have any chance at all. It will be better if the parents are here to hold him and comfort him. Are they around?'

'The mother will be here in a moment,' Helen told him. 'She's filling in a consent form. We're still trying to contact the father.'

A nurse brought the woman into the room a short time later. She was white-faced with shock as she stood by the trolley. 'I didn't realise that he had taken the tablets,' she said tearfully. 'I took one with my breakfast this morning, and then the phone rang and I must have left the bottle on the table while I went to answer it. When I got back into the kitchen, Luke was playing with his cars, and I cleared away the breakfast dishes and forgot all about the tablets. I didn't notice that the bottle wasn't on the table any longer. He must have slipped it into his pocket and hidden it from me.'

'It's surprising how devious children can be at times,' Matthew said softly. 'Especially if they think they might be in trouble for something.'

He carefully turned the child onto his left side, ensuring that his head was lower than his stomach. 'If you could hold him securely and speak to him soothingly, it should make this whole process a lot easier for him.'

He spoke to her calmly and reassuringly, and she did as he advised and gently held her child while Matthew put an endotracheal tube in place.

'I've always warned him about tablets,' the woman said. 'I never dreamed he would do something like this.'

'Unfortunately, children don't always know the difference between sweets and certain tablets at this age.'

Sarah was busy setting up an intravenous line. 'Are we giving him desferrioxamine?' she asked quietly.

'That's right, but infuse it slowly, otherwise it could induce hypertension. We'll lower the dosage when he shows signs of improvement. The diarrhoea was bad so he'll need saline, dextrose and potassium supplements, too.'

'I'll see to it.'

She was glad that Matthew was doing the washout and not her. She didn't know whether she could trust herself to cope with a fractious, unhappy child, but Matthew seemed to take it all in his stride. He appeared to have a magic touch with this little boy, as well as being able to deal with the mother's fears and guilt. Although the washout procedure took some time, it went smoothly enough.

'I think we can finish now,' Matthew said. 'We'll get an abdominal X-ray to ensure there are no tablets left in the stomach.'

'Is he going to be all right?' the boy's mother asked.

'We're doing everything we can for him,' he told her. 'We'll need to admit him to hospital so that we can keep an eye on him for the next few hours, because there's always the possibility that other problems might develop. Hopefully we've dealt with this in time, though.'

'Can I stay with him?'

'Yes, of course. A nurse will take you both up to the ward.'

'Thank you.'

Matthew went to change into clean scrubs a few minutes later, while Sarah dealt with the admission form.

When he returned to the desk, she said quietly, 'You were very good with that little boy. Not just with the treatment, but the way you handled him. How did you get to be so instinctive with children?'

'I didn't realise that I was.' His brows drew together. 'My brother has a son, but he's younger than Luke...he's just over two years old. I see him quite a lot these days, so I suppose I'm getting to understand something of the way young children think.'

'I didn't know that you had a nephew.'

'No. Well, it's been difficult to keep in touch. I've been away for quite a while, and although I've managed to get back occasionally to visit my family, you never seemed to be around at the time. I haven't seen Rachel either. Whenever I tried to get in touch, she was always somewhere else, or too busy to meet me.'

That surprised Sarah. Rachel had never mentioned that Matthew had tried to get in touch with her. Had that been because she had been trying to avoid him?

He reached for a chart and scanned the details written there. 'Nicky's a lovely little lad, and I see him as often as I can because I think family is important and I want to keep in contact with them as much as possible. That's one of the reasons I decided to come back here as soon as I was able.'

Sarah sent him a quick look. Matthew had always been close to his family. He thought the world of his parents and he and his older brother had always been a team. Whenever any of them had found themselves with any kind of problem, he had always backed them up. It was only natural, after all, but she couldn't help feeling a ripple of discontent. Matthew's parents had treated her father unfairly, as though the business collapse had been entirely his fault.

'Nicky isn't too well at the moment,' he added. 'He's been having some abdominal problems, but the symptoms are vague and the family doctor hasn't been able to pin them down to anything specific so far. Harry and Laura think he might be complaining because he's worried about starting play school. They've taken him to look around the place a couple of times, but Nicky wasn't too keen.'

'He's still very young. It's a big thing, leaving Mum behind and spending lots of hours in a strange place. It's probably not surprising that he's having tummy problems.'

He sent her a thoughtful look. 'It's the same with adults, I suppose. They react to stress in a similar way.' He signed off the chart and replaced it on the desk. 'How is your father? The other day you said that he hadn't been well.'

'I think he may have angina. We won't know properly until he has tests, but in the meantime I'm trying to get him to take things easy.'

'I can't see your father doing that. Are you still living with him?'

She shook her head. 'No, I have my own place now, a cottage just off the coast road, not far from my dad's. It's only small, but it does for me. Rachel is staying at the house with him.'

'Is she? What happened to the flat? I thought she liked living there. She said it was central and she liked the freedom and the sense of being close to where everything was happening. Did she get tired of sharing it with students? Or has she moved in with your father so that she can keep an eye on him? I suppose that would be the best idea.'

'As it turns out, yes, it is a good idea. At least I feel happier, knowing that Dad has someone to watch out for him.' She wasn't going to tell Matthew that Sarah couldn't afford the flat now that she had a child to look after.

The more she thought about it, the more she was convinced that Matthew must be Emily's father. How would he react if he was to learn that he had a daughter? Sometimes she thought that Rachel was too stubborn for her own good. Her reasons for not divulging the name of the father of her child didn't make any sense, but Rachel could be every bit as determined as James Carlisle when it came to a matter of pride and self-sufficiency.

'I'll have to give her a call as soon as I get some free time,' Matthew said musingly. 'I've been really busy lately, starting this new job, but it would be good to see her again and talk over old times. We've a lot of catching up to do.'

More than you could possibly imagine, Sarah reflected inwardly, but she wasn't going to voice her thoughts aloud. Ought she to warn Rachel that Matthew was back?

Sarah wasn't sure what to do. She was protective of her sister, and she didn't want to see her hurt, but perhaps it would be better to let Matthew make the first approach. That way, she wouldn't have pushed

either of them into anything, and getting back together again would be purely down to Matthew's ef-
forts. Wouldn't Rachel feel better for that?

The prospect of the two of them meeting up again
was troubling. It was probably bound to happen,
sooner or later, and there was no knowing how things
would go between them.

As to herself, she didn't know how she would feel
if they got together again. For a long time she had
not wanted to even contemplate the idea, because it
would signify the end of all her secret hopes and
dreams, and now that it was imminent she was deeply
troubled. She had buried her emotions in a dark and
hidden place and it was intolerably painful now to
have them dragged out into the open.

CHAPTER THREE

'SARAH, would you come and have a look at Mrs Lawrence for me?' Helen said. 'I'm quite worried about her. Her blood pressure's way off the scale and I'm afraid that she might be heading for a stroke.'

Sarah nodded. 'Of course.' She had been working in A and E for a couple of weeks now, and she knew that Helen wasn't one to worry unduly. If Helen thought that something was wrong, it needed to be investigated right away. 'Do you know of anything that might have brought on the episode?'

'I think she just had an upset at home—something to do with her son going off the rails. They had an argument, but it all got out of hand apparently. He was the one who brought her in this afternoon. He said he was frightened by the way she suddenly crumpled. To be honest, I think he's feeling guilty about having brought this on. He says she's had episodes like this before.'

'Perhaps she's worrying about him unduly. He can't be too bad, if he took the trouble to bring her to hospital.' Sarah followed the nurse to the curtained-off bay where the patient was being assessed.

Jenny Lawrence was lying on the bed, looking very pale and in a state of collapse. She had been sick, and when Sarah examined her she found that her skin was clammy to the touch.

'I feel so ill,' the woman said with an obvious effort. 'My head hurts so much. What's happening to me? I'm going to die, aren't I?'

'Not if I have anything to do with it,' Sarah said with a reassuring smile. 'Try to stay calm and relax, Jenny. I'm just going to run my stethoscope over you for a moment.'

'Where is my son?' Jenny asked in an urgent whisper, struggling to get her breath. 'I didn't mean to scare him. I got so angry, it all just blew up out of nothing.' Sarah frowned. Talking was making her condition deteriorate, but she obviously needed to settle this problem in her mind.

'I sent him to go and get a cup of tea,' Helen said. 'Then he's going to sit in the waiting room until we've finished looking at you.'

The woman seemed to calm down a little at that, and Sarah continued to listen to her chest. The heart rate was rapid, she discovered, along with her pulse, and Sarah said quietly, 'OK, that's all done, you can lie back now. I just want to examine your tummy, and then I can let you rest again.'

When she had finished, Sarah told her, 'I'm going to get the nurse to give you some oxygen to help you breathe more easily. We'll give you something to lower your blood pressure, and you need to rest here for a while. I'll be back shortly.'

She left the woman with Helen, and went in search of Matthew. Something about this case bothered her.

He was with a patient, but when she asked if she could have a word with him, he handed over to another doctor and came to speak to her.

'Problem?' he queried.

'Yes. I have a patient who is suffering from hypertension. I thought at first, because she's had episodes like this before, that it might just be stress that was bringing it on, and that things would settle down and I could treat it in the usual way. I don't think it's as simple as that, though. She looks too ill, and I think there may be something more behind it. I'm just not sure what I should be looking for.'

'You're probably wise to be cautious. You should always follow your instincts. If you think there's something more wrong with her, then there probably is. Have you done blood and urine tests?'

'I did. There's glucose present in the urine, but I don't believe she's diabetic.'

'Hmm. You need to do a 24-hour urine-screening test. Do a CT scan of the abdomen and get a chest X-ray. In the meantime, you can give her labelatol by mouth to bring the blood pressure down.'

'I'll do that.' She hurried back to her patient, prescribed the medication and sent her for a CT scan and chest X-ray, as Matthew had advised.

He caught up with her a little later in the doctors' lounge. She had just been helping to treat a man who had been injured in a traffic accident, and she had managed to stand in the wrong place just as one of his arteries had spurted. There was a slight spatter of blood on her cotton top, and now she was staring into her locker, searching for a change of clothes.

She turned around when she heard Matthew come into the room.

He flicked a glance over her. 'I hope the patient came out of that better than you did.'

She nodded. 'He's doing all right now. I wanted to change into something clean, but I seem to have forgotten to bring another set of clothes with me.' She frowned. It wasn't like her not to make provision for circumstances like this. Lately, though, her mind seemed to be all over the place...not where her work was concerned, but with other things.

Matthew seemed to think so, too. 'That doesn't sound like you. You usually have everything in hand.'

'Not this time, unfortunately.' She was all too conscious that he was watching her, his blue eyes travelling over her, missing nothing, and it suddenly occurred to her that she was most likely staring at the very source of her troubles. Ever since Matthew had come back to his home town, she had gone adrift. It was as though her mind had tumbled into a state of mild chaos, and her wits had been scattered all over the place.

'I could lend you a shirt of mine, if you like,' he offered, going over to his own locker and riffling through the contents. He held out a pale blue shirt to her, made of soft cotton. 'If you roll up the sleeves, it should serve until you get home. You've only a couple of hours left before the end of your shift,

haven't you, and then you could change into something of your own?'

She nodded. 'Yes, that's true.'

'There you go, then. Now you're all fixed up.'

She nodded absently, frowning, and he said,
'You're looking very thoughtful. Is there another
problem?'

'No, not really. I've just remembered that I meant
to ask at Reception for a local bus timetable.'

'Oh? Why do you need one of those?'

Sarah winced. 'My car went in for a service and
should have been back yesterday, but they found a
problem that they needed to deal with. I got a lift in
this morning, but Rachel couldn't manage it this afternoon, so I'm taking the bus home.'

'I could drop you off,' Matthew said. 'You said
that you didn't live far from your father's house,
didn't you? That's on my way home.'

His offer was unexpected, both of the shirt and the
lift. Flustered, she accepted the shirt from him, and
said, 'Actually, I was going to pop in and see my dad.
He wasn't very well again this morning, according to
Rachel, and I want to make sure that he's all right.'

'That's OK. No problem.' He sent her an amused
glance. 'Are you going to put that shirt on, or are you
just going to stand there and hold it up in front of
you for the rest of the day?'

She gave a small jump. 'I'll put it on,' she managed. There was a screen at one side of the room and
she disappeared behind it, quickly shrugging off the

ruined top she was wearing and slipping her arms into the shirt.

It fitted her reasonably well, and she did as he had suggested, rolling back the shirtsleeves. It felt strange, having this garment next to her skin. It smelled fresh and clean, but she was all too aware that it was something that Matthew had worn, and the effect it had on her was unsettling. Her skin heated and a ripple of awareness ran through her like a tide of molten silk. It was like being close to him, having him touch her.

'Is it OK?'

'It's fine, thanks.' She hoped he hadn't heard the faint note of unsteadiness that threaded her voice.

Coming out from behind the screen, she tossed her stained top into a bin. Matthew's glance shimmered over her. 'Yes,' he murmured, 'it looks fine.' He went over to the coffee-pot and poured himself a drink. 'Want one?' he asked.

She nodded. Perhaps it would help to calm her nerves.

'How is your patient with the hypertension?' he said, coming over to her and handing her a mug. 'Did you find anything from the tests?'

'I did. Helen's monitoring her right now, and I was going to come and find you and ask you to take a look at the abdominal film. It looks as though the woman has a tumour on her adrenal gland. I think that must be what's causing the problem.'

'I suspected it might be something like that. These tumours are usually benign, but they secrete hormones in an uncontrolled and irregular way that can raise blood pressure to an alarming degree. She'll need to have surgery, of course. You should put her on an infusion of phentolamine to bring the blood pressure under control.'

'I'll see to it.' She took a sip of her coffee. 'I expect her son will be pleased to learn that he's not the cause of all her troubles. He thought he was adding to her stress and making her ill.'

He made a wry face. 'It happens. Stress can do bad things. You must have seen it for yourself because your father's a case in point, isn't he? Do you think his ill health is due to all the problems he's been having with his business?'

'I'm sure it hasn't helped.'

'What was wrong with him this morning?'

'He was getting palpitations and he was short of breath. When I checked his pulse it was irregular and it didn't correspond with his heart rate, and that worried me. He used his angina spray, and that seemed to settle things down, but I've told him that he needs to go and see his GP and get him to bring his hospital appointment forward. I'm afraid that he has some kind of heart disease that will only worsen with time, and I think he needs to go on digoxin to control his heart rate.'

'You're probably right, but do you think there's any chance he'll do as you suggest?' Matthew looked sceptical. 'He can be difficult at times, can't he? It's not always possible to get through to him.'

Sarah leapt to her father's defence. 'He can be set in his ways, I'll admit. He doesn't like to own up to any frailty. He maps out a course for himself and tries to see it through, and he's not at all happy if he has to deviate from it. I don't really see that as a fault, though. I see it more as being purposeful. He had a vision in mind when he set up the business, and he didn't want anything to turn him away from it. It's only because of his dogged determination that he's managed to keep going these last few years.'

'That's true enough. A lesser man would have given up when his partner ran off with the bulk of his capital, but not your father. He kept on going even when the odds were set against him.'

'You mean when your parents turned on him?' She said it with a bite. It was a sore point, even after all these years.

'That isn't what I meant and they didn't turn on him,' he answered tersely. 'Perhaps you should try to see things from their point of view. They had invested a lot of money in the business, and they lost everything. They were upset and angry, and surely that was a natural reaction? How could you expect them to behave otherwise? Did you think they would simply shrug and say, "OK, that's life"?'

'No, of course not. But they blamed him for something that wasn't his fault.'

'They thought that he should have seen it coming. He obviously didn't know what his partner was really like, and that made him a bad judge of character.'

'In their eyes...but I knew that you agreed with them. You stood by your parents even though my father was shattered by what happened and by the

way they turned on him. I just think he was too trust-
ing, that's all. Anyway,' she added in a clipped tone,
'he's paying back everything that your parents are
owed, with interest. It's taking some time, I grant you,
but I don't see that he can do any more to try to put
the situation right. He's worked hard to get back on
his feet, and I'm proud of him.'

'I agree, he's doing what he can to put things right.
Look, Sarah,' he said seriously, 'I think we have to
put all this behind us once and for all. If we don't,
it's simply going to go on festering, and it will get in
the way of everything. You and I have to work together. We can't go on sniping at each other like this.'

'That's easy for you to say, isn't it? It didn't affect
you the way it did us. The floor didn't cave in beneath
your feet. You simply collected your things together
and walked away.'

His jaw tightened. 'I did what I could, what I felt
I needed to do at the time, and then I got on with my
life. There was nothing else to be done.'

'If that's how you feel, then there's no point in
talking about this any more, is there?' Her mouth
made a bitter line. She put her mug down in the sink
and headed for the door. 'I have to go and see to Mrs
Lawrence,' she muttered. 'I need to explain to her
about the tumour.'

'I'll come and look at the abdominal film before
you do that,' Matthew said.

'As you please.'

Jenny Lawrence was clearly taken aback by the
news when Sarah broke it to her a few minutes later,

but she said quietly, 'At least it helps to know what's causing the illness. I was living a nightmare before.'

'Will she be all right? After the operation, I mean?' Anthony, her son, asked huskily. 'You said that these things are usually benign, didn't you?' He reached for his mother's hand and clasped her fingers gently, in a way that said he was going to be there for her, come what may.

Sarah said gently, 'These things usually turn out very well once the tumour has been removed. I'm really pleased that we've found out what was causing this.'

'Thanks, Dr Carlisle,' Anthony said. 'My dad will be relieved, too, when he gets back from Scotland. I phoned him to tell him what was happening, and he was very worried. He's on his way back now, and he should be here in a couple of hours.'

'That's good.' She smiled at Jenny. 'We'll make arrangements to admit you to a ward, so that we can keep an eye on you for a while.'

She left them, satisfied that mother and son were happily reconciled. After that, she spent some time clearing up all the loose ends left over from the rest of the day before she realised that it was time for her shift to end. She went to get her jacket from the doctors' lounge.

'Are you ready to go?' Matthew asked, putting his head round the door.

She stared at him. In the intervening rush of work, Sarah had forgotten that he had offered her a lift. She was still feeling uptight after their earlier conversation, but she could hardly back out now, could she? He looked as though he had got over it.

She hesitated momentarily, and he lifted a dark brow. 'Yes, I'm ready,' she murmured. 'I'll just get my bag.'

'Are you in a hurry to go straight home?' he asked, and she looked at him in surprise. 'It's just that I bought a new house a couple of months ago, since I'm going to be staying in the area. I'm not properly settled in yet, and I'd appreciate your advice about some of the alterations I'm planning on making—and about the furnishings, too. You'd be doing me a great favour. It's on the way, and it shouldn't take too long.'

His expression was hopeful, and she nodded agreement. 'All right.'

He wanted her input, and it would be a way of thanking him for the lift. That way she wouldn't be beholden to him in the future. 'I expect Dad won't be home for at least another hour anyway. He usually works later on a Monday evening.'

Matthew raised a dark brow. 'He still goes in to work, then, even though he's unwell?'

She nodded. 'You know my dad. He never gives in.' She made a face. 'I asked his secretary to let me know if he showed any signs of a relapse. At least I know that I can rely on her to keep him in line.'

He made a brief smile. 'Let's go, then, shall we, if you're ready?'

The journey to his house only took a few minutes, and when Matthew parked his car on the cobblestone drive and she stepped out to look around, Sarah was startled by what she saw. She had been expecting something modern and functional, perhaps along the lines of his parents' home, but this was nothing like that.

This house was tucked away in a little valley, just a mile or so from the coast, nestling against a background of mature trees and fronted by an expanse of rich green turf. Haphazard banks of flowering shrubs were set amongst low, wide terraces, with moss-covered steps leading to the front of the house.

It was built of stone, with a broad expanse of Georgian windows and a slate roof the same colour as the stonework. It was bathed in evening sunlight now, which cast a muted sand-coloured glow over everything. She had never seen anything quite so beautiful.

'What do you think of it?'

'I think it's absolutely lovely. I had never imagined that you would choose anything like this,' she said softly.

He lifted an amused brow. 'You think I'm a philistine, don't you—that I don't know how to appreciate the finer things of life?'

'I wouldn't put it quite like that. It's always seemed to me that you prefer to have everything in its place, thoroughly organised and streamlined, so that you can be efficient in whatever you do and not have to waste any time. This house looks as though it's more about relaxation, summer teas out on the terrace and generally being able to take time to wind down.'

His mouth curved in a smile. 'That's exactly what I wanted. In the work we do, we have to be clear-thinking, make on-the-spot decisions, weigh things in the balance from moment to moment. Here, I want to get away from all that. I suppose I wanted a kind of haven, somewhere I could come home to and forget the worries of the day.'

'Then I think you've chosen perfectly.'

'Come and see the inside. You may not like that quite so much. Generally the rooms are reasonably sized, but the kitchen is small and a touch cramped and I'm not sure what to do to make it right. I've always thought the kitchen should be the heart of the house.'

Inside the house, the rooms were filled with light. The living room was spacious, with two French doors opening out onto a large garden. There were two comfortable sofas and a low, glass-topped coffee-table, and to one side of the stone fireplace there were shelves lined with books.

'I like this,' she said turning to him. 'I like the way that you've furnished it, and I love the feeling of space and the way that the light pours in through those doors.'

He nodded. 'It's my favourite room, too. I like being able to look out over the garden. I've put a bird table just beyond the patio, close to the little water fountain, and I can sit in here and watch the birds as they come for food or to have a bath when it gets hot.'

She came over to the windows to look. 'I see what

you mean,' she murmured. 'Look, there are some chaffinches on the table now.' Smiling, she turned around to share with him what she was seeing, and all at once she collided with him. She hadn't realised that he'd been so close, looking over her shoulder, and now, for an instant, his long body tangled with hers and she felt a flood of awareness fill every part of her being. Her soft curves were crushed against his strong frame, and her heart began to thud wildly in response to his nearness. A sensation of heat shot through her from head to toe.

'I was…' she began. 'I mean, I thought…'

'I'm sorry.' Matthew drew back, putting up his hands in a gesture of withdrawal, flattening his palms as though a pane of glass had sprung up between them. 'It was my fault.' He took another step away from her, as though he needed the assurance of safe distance.

Sarah didn't move. She was still waiting for the erratic beat of her pulse to calm down. Matthew hadn't been affected in the same way that she had been, had he? He still looked perfectly cool and in control of himself, whereas she was all over the place.

She had always been attracted to him, had always longed for his touch, and it just went to show that nothing had changed. The intervening years while he had been away had done nothing to lessen her feelings towards him.

He lowered his hands. 'I'm glad that you like the living room,' he said. 'Come through to the kitchen, and see what you think of that.'

His manner was faintly brisk and she guessed that he wanted to be on the move again. It was easy for him to put this fleeting moment of consciousness behind him, wasn't it? He had always thought of her simply as a friend, never as anything more. Sarah was the one who had the problem of reconciling herself to the way things were.

He led the way, ushering her into a small, square room, which was bordered on three sides with cupboards and appliances. She pulled herself together and looked around. She noticed that there was an annexed room beyond, through a wide archway. Walking through the arch, she saw that the adjoining room was a conservatory with windows on three sides looking out over the garden.

She turned back to the kitchen. 'I think you're right about this being too small,' she said. 'What kind of changes did you have in mind?'

'I thought maybe I could fit some of the appliances into the cupboard space. That might give me a little more room, and I could perhaps put in a breakfast bar. As it is, at the moment there's nowhere to sit and eat, but the dining room is too far away from here to be practicable.'

She put her hand on the wall that housed most of the cupboards. 'What's on the other side of this wall?' she asked.

'A utility room of sorts. There's mostly junk in it at the moment.'

She went and looked at the room. 'If I were you,' she said thoughtfully, 'I would knock down the wall between the kitchen and utility room to make it into one big kitchen, and I would use the conservatory as a dining area. I imagine it would be lovely to sit and eat in there and enjoy the sunlight.'

He mused on that for a moment. 'I hadn't thought of that. You're right, of course. It's the perfect answer.' He gave her a wide smile. 'Thanks, Sarah.'

'You're welcome.'

They checked out the upstairs rooms, but Sarah didn't want to linger in the main bedroom. She didn't want to think about him settling down here at night. She didn't want to think about him in bed at all. It raised far too many conflicting emotions in her.

'I'm not sure what to do about the windows in here,' he said. 'They're very tall and fairly wide, and I think they need some special treatment to make the room look good, but I've no idea what would be best.'

'I would go for long curtains, floor to ceiling, with tie-backs and a carefully designed pelmet to make the most of them,' she said. 'I think a simple design would be ideal, so as not to detract from the rest of the room. But Rachel would know better than me about that. Fabrics are her thing, and she has a flair for design. I'm sure she would be able to advise you.'

He nodded. 'She used to show me her designs when she was at college. She certainly has a talent for that kind of thing.' He led the way down the stairs. 'Shall I make coffee for us? Perhaps you'd like something to eat?'

Sarah checked her watch. 'I'd better not,' she murmured. 'Dad will be back from work by now, and I want to check up on him before I go home. Usually, I try to pop in and see him on my way to work, but that was impossible today.'

'That's all right. We'll leave now. It won't take us more than five minutes to get to your father's place. Is Rachel likely to be there?'

Sarah nodded. 'I expect so. She had to go and visit a sick friend on the other side of town, but I imagine she'll be home by now.'

'Good. Perhaps, if she hasn't made any plans, we'll be able to chat for a while.'

They walked out to his car, and Sarah was quiet, suddenly anxious about that meeting. Was she doing the right thing in drawing him and Rachel back together again? How would he react when he saw Emily for the first time? More to the point, how would Rachel respond?

As to her own feelings, she pushed them away and buried them firmly out of sight.

CHAPTER FOUR

'GOOD heavens. Matthew, I had no idea that you were back.' James Carlisle was obviously startled to see Matthew standing on his front doorstep. He sent him a faintly strained glance, and then said, 'How long have you been here in Devon? Are you going to be around for long?'

'I'm back for good, actually,' Matthew murmured. 'I'm working at the hospital, in A and E, and I've just bought a house close by.' He glanced obliquely at Sarah, who was standing by his side. 'I take it Sarah hasn't brought you up to date, then?' His eyes darkened momentarily, and Sarah guessed that he was weighing up the reasoning behind her omission.

She immediately felt uncomfortable. She had always meant to mention it to her father and Rachel before too long, but she hadn't wanted to stir things up, and then it had been too late and she'd let the opportunity slip by.

James shook his head. 'Not that I recall.' He was frowning, but now he said, 'Come in, won't you? I'm sorry, I didn't mean to leave you hanging around on the doorstep. I don't know why Sarah didn't let you in. She has her own key.'

'We were talking,' Sarah said, 'about the way

you've redesigned the front garden. I was just going to get my key when you opened the door.'

'Ah.' He nodded. 'I heard the car pull up and came to see who it was. I knew yours was still at the garage.'

They followed him into the house. Sarah was relieved that no immediate tension had sprung up to spoil this meeting. If her father had any reservations about Matthew being there, he was hiding them well enough.

The truth was, she hadn't known quite what to expect when Matthew and her father finally came face to face again. Before the problems with his ex-partner had arisen, and the coolness between himself and Matthew's parents had erupted, Matthew had always been a welcome visitor.

'I imagine a few things have changed around here since you left,' her father was saying.

'Some,' Matthew commented. 'They've built a new bypass, and a few more houses have sprung up here and there. This place is much the same as I remember it, though. Except that it looks as though you've given the front a fresh coat of white paint recently, the shutters, too. It's looking good. Have you had the thatch on the roof renewed as well?'

'I had that done after winter ended. The shutters are Sarah's handiwork. She insisted that they would look good if we painted them a bright, sunshine yellow. I must say that I had my doubts, but she proved me wrong in the end. To be honest, I don't know how she finds the time to fit everything in when she has a house of her own to keep her occupied these days.'

Matthew smiled. 'It's looking beautiful now that the flowers are all in bloom but, then, it always was a pretty cottage.'

Her father led the way to the living room. 'Rachel's sitting out there on the terrace,' he said. 'We were just enjoying a cool drink before the sun goes down. Come and join us. Have dinner with us, if you like.'

Matthew gave him a cautious look. 'I wouldn't want to put you to any trouble,' he demurred. 'Anyway, I shouldn't stay too long. I have some things to sort out back home.'

'It's no bother. Rachel has made a salad, and I'm sure there'll be plenty to go around. Sarah, you'll be staying, won't you? Rachel was hoping that you would.'

She nodded. It would give her time to see how her father was really doing. He looked well enough, just now, but given his recent bouts of ill health, she wanted to be certain.

'Good. Come on, then, both of you.' He walked out onto the terrace, and said, 'Rachel, we have a visitor.'

Rachel turned around, about to get to her feet, but then she halted, obviously taken aback to see who it was who had arrived. She faltered, then recovered herself after a moment or two and stood up.

Sarah couldn't see any sign of Emily in the garden, but she guessed that she wouldn't be too far away.

'Matthew,' Rachel said huskily. 'I didn't know that

you were coming home.' She looked at him guardedly. 'Is this a flying visit? Are you back here to see your parents?'

'No, as a matter of fact, I'm here to stay.'

Tension had sprung up between them and Sarah couldn't stand the wary atmosphere for a moment longer.

'This is all my fault,' she said awkwardly. 'I should have told you before this, but everything's been in a bit of a turmoil just lately, what with me starting this new job and with Dad not being well, and one thing and another. Matthew's the consultant in A and E where I'm working.' Her voice trailed off. She wasn't convincing anybody. She should have told them, not brought him to them this way. It was no wonder that they were shocked.

Matthew said softly, 'How have you been, Rachel? How's life been treating you?'

'I'm doing all right,' she said. There was still a thread of caution in her voice.

'I heard that you gave up the flat. That must have been a wrench.'

'Not really. I'd outgrown it and, besides, I wanted to be here to keep an eye on Dad.'

'Yes, that's what Sarah said.'

Sarah glanced at him. Did he have his doubts about the reason she had given him? He was nobody's fool, and it wouldn't take him long to guess that there was more going on here than he was being told.

A child's voice sounded from around the corner of the house. 'Not fly 'way. You stay there.'

Matthew frowned, and Rachel suddenly went pale.

Emily appeared, holding out her hand. 'Look, Mummy,' she said happily. 'It's a ladybird.'

'So it is,' Rachel said. 'You must be careful to keep your hand open, Emily, so that you don't hurt it.'

'It was on the flowers,' Emily confided, 'but I putted my hand out, and he climbed on.' She giggled.

Matthew watched the exchange, an expression of incredulity on his face.

He made a slight sound in his throat, and Emily turned and saw him for the first time. Her little mouth dropped open and she sidled closer to her mother.

'Who 'at man?' she whispered.

Rachel hesitated. 'A friend,' she said after a moment.

Her father cleared his throat. 'I'll go and organise some food for us,' he said. 'Make yourself comfortable, Matthew. I'm sure that you and Rachel have a lot to talk about.'

Matthew nodded, still looking bemused. He glanced at Rachel's hands, and Sarah guessed that he was looking for a ring. He didn't find one.

'Hello, Emily,' he said, giving her a smile. 'You have your mummy's pretty curls, and her blue eyes, too.'

Emily shook her head. 'Not Mummy's. Mine,' she said with a pout.

Matthew chuckled. 'Of course they are. My mistake.' He glanced up at Rachel. 'I didn't realise that you had a child,' he said softly. 'How old is she?'

'Three and a bit,' Rachel said on an unsteady note.

She looked at him, and there was a hint of fear in her eyes, as though she was afraid that he would ask more.

Sarah decided that it was time she left them on their own. She said quietly, 'I think I'll go and help Dad make the tea.'

Neither of them watched her go. She walked into the kitchen, and there was a heavy feeling in the pit of her stomach that she couldn't account for. It had been bound to happen sooner or later, that Rachel and Matthew would meet up again. She had been prepared for it for some time now. She just hadn't expected that she would feel this way, as though she was completely drained, empty of hope.

'You've left them to it, have you?' her father murmured. He was filling the kettle at the sink, and now he set it down and flicked the switch. 'It's been a long time, hasn't it?' He sent her a thoughtful look. 'It must have come as a bit of a shock for you, finding that you were going to be working with him.'

She nodded. 'It did a bit. I'm sorry I didn't mention it before this.'

'Well, you've had a lot on your mind lately.'

Sarah went to the fridge and took out a bowl of salad. It helped her to keep busy. It might stop her from dwelling on the conversation that might be going on outside.

'Does it bother you that he's going to be around?' she ventured after a while. 'I know that relations haven't improved at all between you and his parents.'

He grimaced. 'It's been difficult for all of us, but I

know in my heart that I shouldn't blame Matthew for anything that happened. The sad thing is that I still haven't been able to reconcile the situation with his parents. They've stayed very cool towards us.'

'You're paying them back the money that they lost, with interest. I would have thought that would go some way to make them think differently.'

'Well, it's not to be.' He drew in a ragged breath, as though he was struggling for air. 'As for Matthew, it's perhaps a good thing that he's come back. Rachel hasn't been herself for some time, and he may be the only one who can change that. They always got along well together in the past, before all that business blew up. I shall be keeping an eye on him, though. If he does anything to hurt her, he'll answer to me.'

Sarah went to fetch a crusty loaf from the bread bin. Did her father have the same suspicions about Emily's paternity that she did? She was shocked to discover that her hands were shaking. Raking over past history was never a good thing to do, especially when it threatened to stir up all the emotions that had been suppressed for such a long time.

'Even so,' she said quietly, 'you were very tactful, leaving them alone together. Do you think Matthew might be Emily's father?'

'I've suspected it for a long time. I did ask Rachel outright once, but she wouldn't give me a direct answer. She said that she and Matthew had a very special relationship, and when I asked about Emily, and said that she needed a father, she said that things wouldn't work out. She said our two families were at loggerheads and it wouldn't make for a happy situation. Just talking about it seemed to upset her, and I didn't want to push it.'

'Perhaps they'll work things out, given time.' Glancing at him, Sarah could see that her father was troubled. Perhaps the shock of having Matthew turn up here had been too much for him. She decided to change the subject.

'Anyway, how have you been feeling today?' she asked. He didn't look well, and she was concerned that he appeared to be tired and out of breath. 'Did you manage to get an appointment with your GP?'

'There was no need to bother him,' he said. 'I'm all right. You mustn't worry about me so much, Sarah.' He began to load a tray with teacups and saucers. 'You know, it might be a nice idea to eat outside while the weather is warm.' He added cutlery from a drawer. 'Actually, I meant to tell you that I had some good news today. We had an approach from someone who was interested in seeing if we could design some equipment for him.'

'That's good,' she murmured. She wasn't fooled by his apparently jovial manner. She knew what he was trying to do. He was hoping that she would be diverted from talking about his problems, but she wasn't going to let him get away with it. 'So you haven't made any arrangement to see your GP again?'

'There wasn't time. I had to pull out all the stops for this new commission. The client may decide to go elsewhere, and I need to make a good impression.'

'I'm sure you will. But you won't get anywhere if

you neglect your health, will you? You really need to have this hospital appointment brought forward. Your health is important, and you can't pretend that it will all turn out all right if you try to ignore it.'

'I know…I know. I will get around to it some time, I promise.' He glanced around at the table, and then went to the fridge and brought out a plate laden with sliced meats. 'I'll make a start on taking some of this food outside,' he said.

Sarah accepted defeat gracefully, for the time being. She would tackle this problem again some time soon, but in the meantime she helped to carry the food out to the terrace and set it out on the table.

Rachel and Matthew had been deep in earnest conversation, from the looks of things. There was almost a secretive look about them, Sarah thought. Now, though, they quickly drew back from each other, and Rachel stood up and began to help with the meal preparations.

'Emily,' she said after a minute or two, 'it's time to wash your hands for tea.' She held her hand out to the little girl and Emily came happily to her.

Matthew watched them walk into the house. 'Emily's a lovely little girl,' he murmured.

'I think so, too,' Sarah agreed, 'but, then, I'm probably biased.'

He gave a wry smile. 'Is Rachel coping with everything? She says she is, but I can see that things aren't quite right with her. She's putting up a good pretence, but she isn't the woman I remember. The spark just doesn't seem to be there any more.'

Sarah sent Matthew a quick glance. He was still as perceptive as ever but, then, he had known Rachel very well. 'It's been difficult for her, bringing up a child on her own. I suppose it's only natural that she isn't the same footloose and fancy-free girl that she once was. I expect things might have been different if the father had stayed around.' It was a barb aimed in his direction but, although he gave her a narrowed look, he didn't rise to it.

Over the next half hour as they sat and ate their meal out on the terrace, Sarah realised that Rachel couldn't have confided in Matthew completely. If he was Emily's father, she still wasn't admitting to it. It was a worrying situation, but perhaps she needed more time to get used to the idea that he was back for good before she said anything.

Emily was growing restless. 'G'anad,' she said in a wheedling tone, tugging at her granddad's hand, 'me want dig garden. See flowers.'

James gave her an affectionate look. 'You mean you want to dig up the seeds that you planted last week to see if they're still growing?'

Emily nodded eagerly.

'You've done that twice already. At this rate they will never grow.'

'Please, G'anad,' Emily insisted.

'Oh, all right, then.' He gave in with good humour, and followed her down the garden path.

Matthew watched them go. 'I've promised that I'll look after my nephew tomorrow,' he said. 'Harry and Laura have to take the dog to the vet for an operation, and they're afraid that Nicky will be upset to see him go.'

'Is this the dog they had before—the golden retriever?' Rachel asked.

'Toby, yes, that's right. He was having some problems, showing signs of sudden weakness, and his abdomen was swollen, so they asked the vet to take a look at him. The scans show that there's a tumour on the spleen, so he's arranged to operate tomorrow to remove it. These things can be benign, so we're hoping the outlook will be positive. They don't want Nicky to be around when all this is going on, though, so I've said I'll take him out and about for the day since it's my weekend off.'

He glanced at Rachel. 'Perhaps you and Emily would like to come out with us? I thought we would go to the fairground, and maybe spend some time on the beach. What do you say?'

Rachel appeared to be thrown by the invitation. She hesitated, and then said quietly, 'I don't think so. I said that I would go over to my dad's workshop and help out with the decorating. He's been a little depressed of late, and I thought it might help to cheer him up if his surroundings are a bit brighter.'

She paused, glancing at Sarah. 'I'm sure Emily would love a day out, though. You're free this weekend, aren't you, Sarah? Perhaps you would like to go with them? I know you told Emily that you would take her to the fair one day soon.'

Sarah frowned. Was Rachel trying to steer clear of Matthew? Her reticence was probably only to be expected, but it was worrying all the same. It was clear that it was going to take some time for her to adjust to the fact that he was here and that he might be part of her life once again.

'Are you sure you won't consider going along yourself?' Sarah said. 'I'm sure Emily would rather be with you.'

Rachel shook her head. 'No, she sees me every day, so she won't be put out by not being with me this once. Anyway, I've already made my plans,' she said firmly, 'and she'll be bored if she has to hang around the workshop all day. Besides, I expect you could do with a break. A day of sunshine might do you some good.'

'That sounds like a reasonable idea,' Matthew said. 'How about it?' He looked at Sarah questioningly.

'Me going to fair?' Emily asked, coming back just then and listening in on the conversation. Her eyes were wide as could be. 'Me like fair.'

Seeing the child's excitement, Sarah could hardly disappoint her, could she? It was clear that Rachel was not going to change her mind.

She nodded. 'Yes, if you like,' she said. 'We'll go to the fair with Matthew and Nicky.'

'That's settled, then,' Matthew said. 'I'll come and pick you both up tomorrow from here, shall I?'

'All right.'

He arrived next day, as promised, bright and early, looking so much like the Matthew she remembered from the old days that he took her breath away.

He was totally relaxed, dressed casually in dark

chinos and a cool cotton shirt that was open at the neck. When he greeted them, his smile tugged attractively at the corners of his mouth, and her pulse shot into overdrive.

Nicky was a little shy to begin with, but Matthew introduced him to Emily, and the children soon got to know each other. Emily showed Nicky her new shoulder-bag and let him look in her pink notebook, and very soon she was acting like a little mother hen towards him.

Sarah watched Matthew as he bent to talk to the children and listen to their excited chatter. He was very natural with them, very much at ease.

She found that she was captivated by his dark good looks. Drawn by some strange compulsion, she watched every movement he made, noticed every slight change in his animated features. Then, suddenly, he looked up at her, a faintly quizzical expression in his eyes, and heat pooled in her abdomen.

She looked away, covering her confusion by keeping herself busy, getting the children organised and into the car.

'Who wants candy-floss?' he asked, some half an hour later as they walked through the fairground.

'Me, me,' the children chorused.

He laughed and took them to the stand where a man twirled sticks in the well of the candy-floss machine, before handing one to each child.

Nicky took a huge bite, and grinned as the sticky confection melted and left a pink trace on his mouth and chin. He was a bright little boy, dark-haired and mischievous, with sparkling grey eyes. 'Can we go on the whirly cars now, Uncle Matthew?' he asked.

Matthew nodded. 'Just as soon as you've finished eating that,' he promised.

They began to walk towards the cars, the children chatting to each other the whole time as though they were old friends.

Matthew gave Sarah a sideways glance. 'You're very quiet today,' he murmured. 'I hope you didn't feel that you were railroaded into this. It just seemed an ideal opportunity to get away from the house, and away from the pressure of work for a while. I'm sorry that Rachel didn't feel able to come along. It might have helped to perk her up a bit.'

'I thought so, too, but you know Rachel—once she's made up her mind, there's no moving her.'

He nodded. 'That's true enough. She has an obstinate streak a mile wide, and it can be difficult getting through to her sometimes.' He grimaced, and then appeared to shrug off the thought. 'Not you, though. You've always been a straightforward kind of woman. You tend to speak your mind, and I like that.'

'Do I? You might not always like what I have to say.'

He laughed. 'That's probably true.' His glance shimmered over her. 'Though there are compensations,' he said with a smile, checking out her bias-cut skirt and matching top. 'You're looking very pretty today.'

'Thank you.' She had chosen a floral print outfit, hoping that it would lift her spirits. She hadn't been sure how she would cope today, being so close to Matthew.

'You look like summer sunshine,' he murmured. 'Those colours suit you. They bring out the dark gold of your hair and the blue of your eyes.' His gaze became searching. 'In fact, come to think of it, there's something altogether different about you today.'

'It's probably the fact that I'm not wearing green scrubs for once,' Sarah said drily. She wasn't going to take his flattery to heart. It didn't mean anything, did it? She had never been a dazzling beauty. In fact, next to Rachel, she had always felt that she faded into insignificance.

He had never had any problem noticing Rachel, had he? There was nothing unusual in that. After all, her sister had a figure that drew men's eyes, and whatever she wore looked good on her.

He chuckled, but shook his head. 'No, it isn't that. I think it's that the pressure is off you now that you've taken time off from your responsibilities. You look relaxed, and it suits you.'

He studied her for a moment or two. 'As far back as I can remember, you've always been hard at work, making sure that everything runs smoothly back home, even when you were trying to cope with your studies at medical school. You still found the time to keep on top of things, to help your father to make a go of the business and give Rachel a helping hand with all her problems. She may be the older sister, but she always seems to turn to you when she's in trouble, doesn't she?'

That was probably true, but Rachel hadn't been so keen to turn to Sarah when she had found that she was pregnant, had she? Everything had changed then. It had been as though Rachel had suddenly grown up, as though overnight she had realised that life wasn't simply a game.

'She doesn't do that so much these days.'

'No, things have changed for her, haven't they?'

By now they had reached the domed area where the cars were situated. 'Come on, Nicky…Emily, let's climb aboard.' Matthew held the children's hands and helped them into the cars, then turned and held out his hand to Sarah. 'Your turn. In you get.'

She stepped up onto the footboard of the circular car, and it swung round slightly with the movement, throwing her off balance momentarily.

Matthew's fingers closed around hers, and an instant spark of electricity travelled along her arm, startling her. For a moment she was transfixed, unable to move or to think of anything but the fact that he was holding her.

'It's all right,' he murmured. 'I've got you. You won't fall.'

His words brought her to her senses, and she pulled herself together and climbed into the car and sat down next to Emily. Matthew seated himself by Nicky, so that the two of them enclosed both children. They fastened their seat belts, and within a few minutes the ride began.

Soon they were spinning round and round. The children were giggling and squealing with glee, and

Sarah was relieved to see that they were enjoying themselves. As the force of the cars' spinning whirled them around, she found herself pinned back against the back of the seat. Matthew's arm was around the children's shoulders, but they were thrown so close together now that he held her, too. It was exhilarating, this sense of being near to him, of sharing this wild, energising experience.

A few minutes later, they all climbed out of the cars and stepped down on to solid ground once more.

'Me want duck,' Emily said, suddenly catching sight of a stall where children were using sticks with wire loops at the end to capture plastic ducks.

'I thought you might,' Matthew said with a smile. 'Let's go, then.'

The children both tried their luck with the sticks. Sarah watched them angle the wire loops this way and that, and said softly, 'I think they get a prize for just trying, on this stall. It looks as though they'll both be coming away with a plastic crocodile. They've not done badly so far, have they? They've managed to win something on the last three stalls. At this rate we'll be running out of hands to carry everything.'

'You think we have problems,' Matthew said drily. 'Take a look over there.' He laid a hand on her shoulder and turned her around to face the opposite direction. 'Look what that poor man's having to cope with.'

She looked. A young couple were walking along, laden down with plastic hammers as large as them-

selves and a huge pink rabbit that grinned from ear
to ear. She laughed. 'I see what you mean.'

Looking back at him, she lost herself for a moment
in his smiling eyes. They were as blue as the sky
above, and for a moment or two she floated help-
lessly, adrift on a soft current of daydreams. How
would it be if Matthew were to take her in his arms
and promise her that they would be together for ever?
He was all she had ever wanted... Life would be so
wonderful.

Tiny fingers were tugging at her skirt. 'Auntie
Sarah...Auntie Sarah...' Confused, Sarah looked
down, and saw that Emily was desperate to get her
attention.

'What is it, sweetheart? What's the matter?'

'See 'at boy, Auntie Sarah...him climbing.' Emily
waved a hand in agitation. 'Him not s'posed to
climb.'

Sarah glanced where she was pointing. A small boy
was trying to climb up on a carousel. No adult was
paying him any attention.

Nicky frowned. 'Him naughty.'

'You're right. He shouldn't be doing that.' She
started forward, then realised that she couldn't leave
Nicky and Emily.

Matthew was already halfway there. 'I'll get him,'
he called back. 'You stay with the children.'

The child was unlucky, though. Just as Matthew
leapt up onto the boards at the edge of the roundabout, the child was hit by one of the horses' hooves.

He tumbled down, ricocheting off the roundabout and onto the ground. He lay there, winded.

Sarah pulled in a shocked breath. He had taken a nasty fall onto his shoulder, and she felt sure he must be hurt.

'Let's go and see if Matthew needs any help,' she said quietly to the children.

They were both subdued. 'Him hurt?' Emily asked. She pushed her thumb into her mouth and stared at the boy.

'I'm not sure,' Sarah said. The boy looked to be about five years old.

Matthew helped the boy to sit up. Just then, a man and woman came rushing to his side. The woman cried out, 'Oh, no Sam...What's happened?'

Matthew said softly, 'Is he your little boy?'

She nodded. 'I'm his mother. I just turned my back for a minute...'

'I'm a doctor,' Matthew told her. 'He took a fall onto his shoulder, and he's in pain. I think he may have broken his collarbone.'

'Broken? What makes you think it's broken?' The man ran his fingers distractedly through his hair.

'From the way he's supporting his arm, and the way he's putting his head to one side to relieve the pain.' Matthew turned to Sam and spoke gently. 'What we need to do, Sam, is to put a bandage around your arm so that it won't hurt quite so much.' He looked around, frowning, deep in thought. 'The question is, where are we to get a bandage from?'

Sarah began to rummage in her bag. 'I've got a

scarf in here,' she muttered. 'It should be big enough to make a sling.' She produced it after a moment, and handed it over to him.

'Thanks.' Matthew worked gently, supporting the child's arm so that his fingertips touched the opposite shoulder. Then he folded the square of the scarf to make a triangular bandage, and draped it over the boy's shoulder and under his hand and forearm. He tied the ends in a reef knot at the hollow above his collarbone, and then finished by tucking the ends under the knot to pad it.

'Does that feel a little more comfortable?' Matthew asked.

'Just a bit,' the boy said. He was white-faced, trying his best not to cry, and he was clearly still a little shocked by what had happened to him.

'It would be better if we had another bandage to secure the arm to the chest,' Matthew murmured.

'Would a belt do instead?' the boy's mother asked.

'I should think so,' Matthew said. 'We can give it a try anyway.'

The woman removed her belt from her jeans. 'Here you are.' She watched as Matthew carefully put it around the boy. 'Will he be all right?'

'I think so. These things usually take three or four weeks to heal up, but you should take him to the hospital so that the shoulder can be X-rayed to determine whether there is any other damage. The doctor will advise you, but you should be able to give Sam some medicine for the pain.' He looked up at both of the parents. 'Are you going to be able to get him there?'

The man nodded. 'I've got my car. We'll take him there now.'

'Good.' Matthew turned back to the boy. 'You've been very brave, Sam. Don't worry, you should be feeling better soon.'

Sarah and Matthew watched as the couple walked away with their son. Emily and Nicky were both very quiet, she noticed.

'Right, you two,' Matthew said briskly, 'you were the ones who showed us what the little boy was doing so I think you deserve a treat. What do you say we go and get some ice cream?'

'Yes,' Nicky said. 'Choc'late splodge.'

'Me want strawberry,' Emily said, her eyes widening in anticipation.

'Chocolate splodge and strawberry it is, then,' Matthew announced. 'Let's go and find the ice-cream parlour.'

He glanced at Sarah, his eyes dancing with light. 'If I remember rightly, yours is vanilla with sticky toffee.'

She nodded, surprised that he had remembered. 'That's the one,' she said with a smile.

She walked with him towards the parlour, but some of the sunshine had gone out of her day. Her mood had changed dramatically from the carefree imaginings of half an hour ago. Then she had let herself be seduced by the lure of his compelling blue eyes, and she had even allowed herself to wonder what might have been.

She was living in a fool's paradise, though. Matthew had never wanted her. He had only ever had eyes for her sister, and she herself was only with him at all today because Rachel had refused his invitation.

CHAPTER FIVE

'EMILY, I've told you twice already to clear that mess up,' Rachel said crossly. 'You've got toys all over the floor and somebody will trip over them. I want you to start putting them back in the box.'

Emily's face took on a mutinous expression. 'Me playing with them.' Coming into the kitchen, Sarah could see straight away that trouble was looming. Emily was in a fractious mood, and not at all inclined to do as she was told.

Sarah was on her way to work and had just called in at her father's house to see how everyone was doing. Not well, by the looks of things.

'You're not playing with them any more in here,' Rachel said. 'You've already knocked a cup over and broken it.'

'Was an acc'dent,' Emily screamed. 'You're a nasty, horrible mummy. I hate you.'

Rachel put a hand to her temple and turned away. Sarah could see that she was beginning to find all this too much, and she decided that it was time to intervene.

'I'll help you to put the toys in the box, Emily,' she said. 'As soon as we've done that, you can go and show Grandad the boat you made. He hasn't seen it yet, has he? You put it in my car the other day before he had a chance to look at it. Look, I brought it with me.' She took it out of her bag and showed it to her.

Still sulking, Emily shook her head. Then, obviously thinking about it a little more, she said with a burst of childish optimism, 'Me put it in water?'

'We'll see. Let's get these toys put away first.'

She took Emily into the living room a few minutes later. Her father was sitting by the writing desk, reading through his letters. He was frowning heavily, deeply preoccupied from the looks of things, and from the ashen colour of his features Sarah realised that he was unwell.

When he heard her come into the room with Emily, though, he turned away from his papers and made an obvious effort to shrug off whatever it was that was worrying him.

'Hello, you two. What have you been up to?'

'Emily's brought her boat to show you,' Sarah murmured. It was a flimsy construction, made out of an egg-box lid, a lollipop stick and a piece of paper for a sail, but Emily was happy with it, and that was what mattered.

James admired her handiwork, and Sarah said quietly, 'How are you this morning? You look a bit pale.'

'I'm fine,' he said dismissively. 'I need to get out in the sunshine a bit more, that's all. I'll try taking a lunch-break outside the workshop today. Perhaps I'll sit on the bench underneath the tree and get some fresh air.'

'Could you not think about taking a day off?

You've been working so hard lately, and I'm worried about you.'

'There's nothing wrong with me. Anyway, Rachel's always around to keep an eye on me. You shouldn't trouble yourself so much. As if you both don't have enough to do...I'll be fine, love, I promise.'

She looked at him doubtfully. 'Phone me at work if you need me, won't you?'

'I won't need to. I'll be fine.'

'You're a stubborn old thing, aren't you?' she chided. 'Look, I'm just going to have a quick word with Rachel. She's another one out of the same mould as you. I thought she was looking a bit frazzled this morning.'

He nodded. 'She has a lot on her mind. You go and have a word with her. I'm not going into work for a few minutes yet, so I can look after Emily for a while.'

'All right, if you're sure.' She looked at him doubtfully, but Emily was playing quietly with her boat and didn't look as though she was going to give him any problems.

Going back into the kitchen, Sarah saw that Rachel was slumped in a chair by the table. She looked washed out and unhappy.

'Are things not going too well?' Sarah asked.

Rachel pulled a face. 'We started off on the wrong foot first thing this morning.' She sighed. 'I don't know why everything's going wrong, but it was like this yesterday as well.' Pushing her hair back from her face with her hand, she added, 'I've not been sleeping too well lately, and that leaves me tired and irritable during the day. I don't know what's the matter with me, but I just don't seem to be able to cope these days.'

'Do know why you're not sleeping properly?'

Rachel shook her head. 'I suppose it could be any number of reasons. Sometimes Emily wakes in the night, and that doesn't help. I don't seem to be able to get a grip upon things these days. I feel as though my life is on hold. Everything seems to be upside down, and I don't know where I am. I think it made things worse when Matthew came back.'

'Did it upset you, him coming back?'

'I think it was a shock, seeing him like that. He just turned up out of the blue.'

Guilt washed over Sarah. 'That was my fault. I'm sorry. I should have prepared you.'

'No, that wasn't it. I would have felt like this whether I'd been warned or not. He was part of everything that went on before. Dad was troubled, too. I could see that it stirred up all the old feelings, and now even Matthew's parents have got in on the act again. That hasn't helped. We all used to get on so well.'

Sarah frowned. 'What do you mean—they've got in on the act again? What do Matthew's parents have to do with any of this?'

Rachel rubbed at her forehead as though that might ease a knot of pain there. She looked as though she was near to tears. 'Of course, you haven't heard, have you? How could you have?'

'Heard what?'

'It looks as though the police might have caught up with Casey Morgan, Dad's ex-partner.'

Sarah's brows shot up. 'After all this time? How did that come about?'

'He was abroad—Spain, I think—and he was taken ill and needed to go to hospital. There was some problem with his papers, and once he'd been treated and his condition stabilised, he was sent back to England. Then the police got involved. They came round here yesterday to talk to Dad, and it looks as though they've been to see Matthew's parents as well, since they were also victims.'

'So what's the result of all this?' The more she heard, the more Sarah was beginning to understand why her father was looking so ill.

'I'm not sure. Matthew's parents are annoyed because they think that he might escape prosecution if he's too ill to stand trial. The police aren't sure whether they will be able to go ahead with questioning him, and they say there's some doubt as to whether a man in his condition would be sent to prison. I'm going to have to try to mediate between them and Dad and Matthew's parents, but I don't know how I'm going to manage to do that. I've a headache already, just thinking about it, and there's Emily to look after.'

From the looks of her, Rachel wasn't in any state

to do anything. Apart from the headache, she looked as though she was close to breaking down.

Sarah said gently, 'I could try to arrange for Emily to go to the crèche at the hospital for a while, if that would help. It might give you some breathing space at least. She would enjoy playing with the children there, and I know there are a couple of empty places at the moment. The girl in charge is a friend of mine, and I think she would be agreeable to Emily taking one of those places if it's just for a short time. How do you feel about that?'

Rachel nodded slowly. 'That might give me a chance to sort myself out. I just feel as though I need a little while to get myself together again.'

'All right. Leave it with me and I'll see what I can do.'

Sarah phoned the crèche and arranged to take Emily with her to the hospital.

'There are lots of children for you to play with, Emily,' she told the little girl some time later when they arrived at the hospital, 'and I'm sure you'll enjoy it here. There are all sorts of toys to play with, and heaps of nice things to do.'

Emily looked dubious as she peered into the nursery, but as soon she saw the home corner her mood changed and she headed straight towards it.

'I'm sure she'll be fine,' the nursery nurse said cheerfully. 'If there are any problems, I'll phone through to A and E and let you know.'

'Thanks, Alice.' Turning to Emily, Sarah gave the

little girl a hug and a kiss then said, 'I'll pop in and see you later on when I have my break.'

A few minutes later, she hurried into A and E. She was frowning, mulling over in her mind what was going on at home, whether her father and Rachel would make any headway in talking to the police.

'You're late,' Matthew said, checking his watch. He was wearing an immaculate grey suit, and he looked the picture of a man in control, an authoritative figure. It was also very clear he was not in a good mood, but the last thing she needed right now was to get into an argument.

'I'm sorry about that. I've been as quick as I could.'

'What happened?'

'There were some things I needed to deal with.'

'Such as?'

He was being curt with her and his manner irritated her. She reacted sharply. 'Such as the fall-out left behind after your parents decided to have another go at my father. Had you heard about that?'

He frowned. 'I heard that Morgan had been found. My parents said there was some doubt as to whether he was ever going to be prosecuted. They want to be sure that your father will go ahead and appear as a witness against him.'

'Yes, well, my dad will have to make up his own mind about that. I'm sure he can do without any more pressure being put on him. After all, if the man's going to escape prison, what would be the point of my dad putting himself through all that stress? Anyway, with everything that's happened, I've had to put Emily into the crèche so that Rachel can get on and deal with it. Dad's gone to work as usual because, when all's said and done, he has to earn a living. I don't see why your parents have to interfere. My dad and Rachel have enough to cope with, without them adding to their troubles.'

'Don't you think they suffered in all this, too? Their good name was sullied when they decided to be part of your father's business. They came out of it badly, and lost the respect of some of their friends.'

'Their friends couldn't have been all that worthy, could they,' she said tartly, 'if they turned their backs on them at the first hint of misfortune?'

His mouth tightened. 'I'm not going to stand here and debate the point with you,' he said in a clipped tone. 'This isn't the time or the place for it. We have work to do. There are patients waiting and there's a man in cubicle four who needs your attention right away.'

'Yes, sir,' she said, with a hint of sarcasm. His features darkened ominously but she chose to ignore his fierce expression. 'Why is he here?'

'He's jaundiced, and he's complaining of abdominal pain. He also seems to be a bit disorientated, according to Helen's notes.'

'I'll go and see him now.'

Sarah went to the cubicle and introduced herself to the man. He wasn't very responsive to her questions, and seemed to be more concerned about a problem at home. He kept talking about losing his job and the fact that the house was mortgaged to the hilt. At times his mind wandered and he seemed confused.

She wondered if he'd been drinking. It seemed a little early in the day, but when she checked his notes she saw that he had been treated for alcohol-related problems on a couple of occasions.

'Mr Peterson, I need to examine you so that I can find out exactly where your pain is coming from. Do you understand what I'm saying?'

He didn't answer. 'There are always too many bills to pay. They always want the money straight away. Nobody cares that you've lost your job.'

He was in his late forties, and his skin had a weathered appearance, as though he was used to working outdoors. Looking at him, Sarah doubted that he was in any condition to work.

She carefully examined him, and said, 'I see from your notes that you've had liver problems, Mr Peterson. Have you managed to cut down on the amount of alcohol that you drink?'

'It's hard,' he said. 'A drop of whisky sometimes takes the edge off my worries.'

'Maybe, but I think you'll only do yourself more damage in the end.' He didn't appear to be listening, and she guessed that he was in pain. 'All right,' she said at last, 'I've finished examining you now, so you can lie back and rest. I'm going to ask the nurse to come and take some blood from you so that we can do tests to find out how your liver is functioning.'

He looked at her blankly, and she explained, 'You see, when the liver doesn't function properly, it isn't able to clear all of the harmful substances from your blood, and that's why you're feeling uncomfortable at the moment. I think we may need to give you some antibiotics to help get rid of some of the toxins that are building up in your body.'

She left him with the nurse. While she was waiting for the results of tests she would have time to attend to another patient, and if she got a move on, she might make some headway and make up for her late start.

She had reckoned without Matthew, though. He intercepted her as she headed for the desk.

'I take it you've examined Mr Peterson,' he said. He looked at her closely. 'You're looking harassed. Is there a problem?'

'I don't think so. His case seems fairly straightforward.'

'So, what conclusions have you come to?'

She wondered why he was questioning her, and faintly resented his interference, but she had to accept that she was relatively new to emergency medicine and perhaps he felt it necessary to check up on her— all the more so because she had been in a rush first thing, and possibly he thought she wasn't on the ball.

'I think he's drinking too much and it's causing problems with his liver. He's confused and in pain, and his cheeks are flushed as though he's been drinking already today. I'm waiting for the results of blood tests.'

'Hmm…I wonder—have you thought about doing an ultrasound scan?'

'What would be the point of doing that? He's been

here before for alcohol-related problems. I would have thought the treatment was going to be much the same as before. I'll advise him to give up alcohol and to alter his diet, but in the long run it isn't going to make much difference, is it? If he carries on this way, despite all our warnings, then he'll finish up with a liver that has been completely damaged by cirrhosis.'

His glance narrowed on her. 'You're not very sympathetic towards him, are you? Don't you think his drinking might have something to do with the hand that life's dealt him?'

She made a face. 'I dare say it has, but we all have to cope with problems of one sort or another. My father didn't turn to drink when his world was turned upside down. He just made up his mind to get over it and get on with his life and to try to make a fresh start.'

'Some people aren't as strong-willed as your father. I don't think you're taking full account of your patient's situation. If you hadn't made such a bad start to the day, I think you would be more inclined to look beyond the surface and get to the root of his problems.' His brows drew together in a dark line. 'It isn't like you to be so dismissive, Sarah. I think you should reassess your thinking and do an ultrasound scan on Mr Peterson.'

Sarah grimaced. His tone had been cutting, and it made her consider her actions all over again. It was true that she wasn't usually so peremptory in her dealings with patients. She was usually much more sympathetic, but she had made a false start today with all the upset at home and perhaps she ought to be thankful that he had pointed out her shortcomings. 'What am I looking for?'

'Another cause for his symptoms. You said that his face looked flushed, and I noticed it, too, when he was brought in. It may not necessarily be due to the drinking. You should get the nurses to check on his temperature, because I think he may have a fever, and that could be adding to his confused state. I've checked back through his notes, and I think we should do a few more tests.'

She was subdued. Matthew was a good doctor. She respected him, and she valued his judgement, and although it went against the grain for her to admit it, it bothered her that he thought she had been less than conscientious. 'All right. I'll see to it.'

It was all her own fault that she was being taken to task, and it was a lesson she would take to heart. She should never allow her home life to get in the way of her work.

She did the scan on her patient and frowned at the results. There was clearly a problem here, but she couldn't sort it out until she had the results from the laboratory, and they would take a while longer.

A little later, when there was a lull in the department, she took the opportunity to go up to the crèche to check on Emily. She made sure that her pager was switched on, so that she could be contacted if there was an emergency or if the results of the tests came through.

To her relief, she found that the little girl was playing happily with another child of around the same age.

'Look what me made,' Emily said excitedly. 'Me done painting.'

'That's wonderful,' Sarah acknowledged with a smile. She wasn't quite sure what the various squiggles represented, but it was certainly a colourful piece of work. 'We'll take that home with us to show Mummy later on. She'll love it.'

Emily beamed her delight. She was happy enough in the nursery, and at least that was another worry off Sarah's mind. 'I have to go back to work now,' she said after a while. 'I'll come and see you again this afternoon.'

When she went back to A and E, the test results on Mr Peterson were back from the laboratory. She studied them carefully, then went and sought Matthew's advice.

'I'm a little worried about Mr Peterson,' she told him. 'I've just been to have another look at him, and his condition is deteriorating rapidly. The liver-function tests suggest a problem. There's also an infection present, and that appears to be the source of his fever.' On a note of apprehension, she added, 'I think there may be a septicaemia so I've put him on supportive therapy, but I'm not quite sure what I'm dealing with here. The scan appears to show an obstruction of some sort.'

'Let me see.' He studied the test results, and then went with her to examine Mr Peterson.

Taking her to one side afterwards, he said, 'I be-

lieve he has a blockage of the bile ducts. The best
way to find out where exactly the obstruction is would
be to inject a contrast medium into the ducts, but from
his condition I doubt we can do that just yet. It looks
as though the infection is suppurative and needs urgent decompression. You had better call a surgeon
and get him to do the procedure right away. In the
meantime, put your patient on an intravenous infusion
of cefuroxime. You should give him metronidazole as
well. Once we get the infection under control, his
condition should start to improve.'

Sarah was shaken by the rapid turn of events. Her
face drained of colour, she hurried away to refer Mr
Peterson to a surgeon, and she was relieved when Ray
Finley arrived in quick time to take him up to Theatre.

She turned her attention to her other patients, but
her mind was on Mr Peterson the whole time. If it
hadn't been for Matthew, she would have missed the
diagnosis entirely, and the consequences could have
been grim. They still could.

Ray came and spoke to her some time later. 'I've
put in a cannula to drain Mr Peterson's infected bile
ducts,' he told her. 'It's a good thing we got into him
in time—any more delay and he could have gone into
septic shock. As it is, he'll need to be admitted so
that we can keep an eye on the infection and find out
exactly what's causing the obstruction. It's probably
stones, but we'll remove those when things have settled down.'

'Thanks for letting me know.'

She watched Ray leave a minute or so later, and

then she turned towards the doctors' lounge. She was shattered by what had happened. With any luck, no one else would be in the lounge, because she desperately needed a moment alone to be able to think things through and to try to regain her composure.

'Are you all right?' Matthew followed her into the room and shut the door.

She shook her head. 'No, I don't think I am. I nearly killed that man. I was so sure that it was just another case of alcoholism.' She lowered her head and sagged back against the wall. 'I feel terrible, thinking what might have happened.'

He came and stood beside her. Tilting her chin so that she had to look at him, he said softly, 'It was a mistake anyone could have made. Cholangitis is a rare cause of cirrhosis. You mustn't blame yourself.'

'But I do,' she said brokenly. 'You didn't miss it, did you? You knew that we needed to delve deeper, and if it hadn't been for you the man might have died. I can't forgive myself for the way I behaved.'

'You haven't had the experience that I have,' he said. 'You're still learning, and that's why I'm here, to make sure that you continually reassess your actions. There is no point beating yourself over the head about it. Junior doctors sometimes make mistakes, and ultimately they have to rely on senior staff to keep them on the right track.'

'I'm just glad I have you to watch over me,' she said huskily. 'I trust you, and I know that you're a good doctor. You made me think twice about what I was doing. I was badly wrong this morning.' She bent her head in shame, feeling almost tearful.

He slid his hand around the back of her head and drew her to him. His fingers tangled in her silky curls. 'Hey, come on. Don't get upset. You listened, that's the main thing.'

'Only because you made me.' She didn't deserve to be held like this, to be able to take pleasure in the comfort of having him near, her head resting against his chest so that she could feel the steady, reassuring thud of his heartbeat beneath her cheek.

Even so, she was glad that he was holding her, and she cherished every moment. It felt so good to be close to him, to feel his arms around her, stroking her gently and easing away some of the tension from her body.

'Thank you for putting me on the right track,' she mumbled after a while.

'You're welcome.' He reluctantly drew back from her. 'I have to get back to work,' he said, giving her a rueful smile.

'Yes, of course. I'm sorry...' The moment was gone, and all at once she felt empty, as though she had lost something very precious. 'I'll follow you in a minute.'

'There's no rush. Take some time to get yourself together.'

She did as he suggested. For the rest of her shift, she was kept busy, and there was no more time to stop and talk to Matthew.

Finally, at the end of what had seemed like a long

day, she set off for home with Emily, calling in on Rachel and her father.

'We're back,' she said in a cheerful tone. 'I think Emily's had a good day. How have things gone for you two?'

'Not too bad.' Rachel gave Emily a welcoming hug. 'Did you like it at the nursery?' she asked.

Emily nodded. 'I made you a picture, see? It's you and Ga'nad. You're in the garden, picking flowers.'

'That is beautiful,' Rachel said. 'I shall put it up on the fridge so that we can all see it.'

Rachel was making an effort, Sarah could see that, but she also recognised that nothing much had changed. Rachel's voice was a little high-pitched and she still looked near to tears, close to the edge, as though the slightest upset would shatter her.

Her father didn't look much better. She caught him rubbing at his chest when he thought she wasn't looking, but she knew there was no point in making any comment. He would just shrug it off as usual.

Rachel had been reading a letter when Sarah walked into the kitchen. 'Is that a letter from your friend?' Sarah asked, glancing at the familiar-looking sheet of flowered notepaper on the table. 'She's been ill, hasn't she? Is she feeling any better now?'

Rachel nodded. 'She's thinking of going away for a week to stay at the coast. Her aunt owns a holiday cottage and she's asking if I can go along with her. She doesn't want be on her own, so she's sent me a photograph of the place in case it would tempt me to join her.'

'That sounds like a good idea. You could do with a break.' Since Matthew had returned, Rachel had gone to pieces, and Sarah was worried that she was heading for some kind of breakdown.

'That's what I said,' her father put in, 'but she won't hear of it.'

Rachel shook her head. 'There's no way that I can go to the coast. I have to think about Emily. I couldn't take her with me because Jane needs peace and quiet.'

'I could look after Emily in the evenings,' her father said. 'I'm sure Sarah and I could work something out between us.'

Sarah thought about it. 'She took to the nursery well enough. It's probably good for her to have other children to play with, and I'm close at hand at the hospital. I don't see why you couldn't go away for a week. As Dad says, we'll be able to manage here, and it will do you good to relax for a while. You seem to have been under a lot of strain just lately and a holiday will probably help to make you feel a lot better.'

'I don't know…I'll have to think about it.'

A day or so later, it was all settled. Between them, they had managed to talk Rachel round. Emily's place at the crèche was secure for a while, and once she knew that everything was taken care of, Rachel decided to take advantage of her friend's offer.

Sarah dropped Emily off at the nursery next morning, and kissed her goodbye. 'I'll come and see you at lunchtime,' she promised.

Emily nodded, then looked a little uncertain. 'Why my mummy gone 'way?' she asked.

Sarah felt a lump in her throat. Was the child un-happy?

'Because she's feeling a bit poorly and she needs to rest,' she explained. 'She won't be away for long, just for a few days, and you'll be able to talk to her on the telephone when we get home. We can talk to her every day, if you like. That will be something to look forward to, won't it?'

She looked at Emily, trying to gauge her reaction. 'Perhaps you could make another picture for her. Then you could give it to her when she comes home again.'

'Yes,' Emily said, brightening up. 'Me make pic-ture. Me do cutting and sticking. Alice said so.'

'That's good. You can show it to me when I come to fetch you.'

It was getting late, and it was high time that she was at work, but she waited to see that Emily was settled before she felt able to go down to A and E.

'Have you taken Emily to the nursery again?' Matthew asked.

'Yes, that's right. I'm not late, am I?'

'No. You're not late, but isn't this getting to be a regular occurrence? Why isn't Rachel looking after Emily?'

'She's gone away to the coast for a few days.'

He was frowning now. 'And she's left you to look after Emily?'

'Yes, I said that I would. It's no problem, and a break will do Rachel some good, I'm sure.'

'Don't you think you're taking on too much?

You're not the child's mother, and you have enough to deal with, working here. Not only that, you're constantly worrying about your father and his health, along with all his business problems. Isn't it time that you thought about yourself for a change? You can't go on doing a stressful job and taking on all the weight of your family's problems as well.'

'There isn't a problem,' she insisted, beginning to get cross at the inquisition. 'Anyway, I don't need you to tell me how I should live my life. I've managed perfectly well on my own up to now.'

He shook his head at that. 'I don't think you have. These last few days you've been tired, out of sorts and short-tempered, and it's clear to me that you're taking on far too much. Besides, a child needs her mother. Emily's only three years old, and it must be strange for her not to have her mother around.'

Sarah's brows shot up. Was that what this was all about? Matthew and Rachel hadn't sorted out their personal lives yet and he must wonder about Emily and who it was that she belonged to. He didn't know whether she was his child, or another man's, but he must be mulling over the possibilities in his head. Was he irritated by the way the child's care was being delegated?

'Isn't that a bit rich, coming from you?' she said tautly. 'A child needs a father, too, but Emily doesn't have one, does she? I don't hear you complaining about that.'

His eyes narrowed. 'And your point is?'

'My point is, who are you to be objecting to

Rachel's child-care arrangements, and what would you know about bringing up a child?'

'As much as the next man, I should imagine. I know that the bond between mother and child can be intense. Mothers have a natural understanding of their children. For the most part, they take on the day-to-day care of their infants, and they're much more sensitive to a child's needs than a man might be. I'm not saying that men can't be equally sensitive, but in my experience it's women who do the bulk of the child-rearing. I think Rachel has opted out, and I don't think it's fair on you.'

She glared at him. 'Then all I can say is that it's a good thing that the decision is mine and not yours. Rachel is unhappy, and she needs our support. Someone has to care. If we turn our back on the people who need us, the world would be a sorry place.'

Her mouth tightened. 'I thought you were Rachel's friend. I thought you cared about her. Instead of criticising her, perhaps you would do better to concentrate on dealing with your own responsibilities.'

He looked as though he was startled by her vehemence and took a step back, almost as though she had hit him. Had she touched a nerve?

'What do you mean by that?'

'Work it out for yourself.'

She turned away from him and walked to the desk, conscious that his gaze was fixed on her. Already she was half regretting what she had said, and she guessed that she had probably gone too far, but she was angry and upset and she had no idea how she was to get through to him.

When it came down to it, Rachel was the only one who could sort that situation out, wasn't she? But she was obstinately digging in her heels. If her child's father hadn't been around for the birth, she wasn't going to involve him now.

In a way, Matthew was right. None of this should have been Sarah's problem, but her emotions were hopelessly tangled up with what was going on in his life. Until this state of affairs was sorted out, she was trapped, a prisoner of her love for him. Even she could see that it was making her unbearably cranky and she still had no idea how the situation could be resolved.

CHAPTER SIX

SARAH had been rushed off her feet all day and it looked as though there was still to be no let-up. A patient, a woman in her mid-forties, had been brought in a short time ago suffering from shortness of breath and chest pain, and now, when Sarah had scarcely had a chance to ask about her medical history, it looked as though things were getting rapidly worse.

'What's happening to me? I can't breathe,' Eve Lancaster gasped. She began to cough, and Sarah could see that she was in trouble. The woman's face was contorted with pain.

'OK, just try to keep the oxygen mask over your face,' Sarah said quickly, and Helen hurried to assist. The woman's pain level had obviously increased and Sarah was very worried about her condition.

'Eve, I'm going to give you something to ease the pain,' she told her, 'then we're going to get a chest X-ray and an ECG so that I can find out what's going on here. I suspect that you might have a small blood clot in your lung, and that's why you're so short of breath. What we need to do is to make you feel more comfortable.'

'Do you need any help here?' Matthew asked.

'Yes, please,' Sarah said. She moved away from the bed and spoke to him quietly. 'I suspect that there's a pulmonary embolus, and I'm planning on giving an infusion of heparin to help prevent any further clots from forming. Her condition is getting worse, though, and I'm worried that she may need urgent surgery.'

He nodded. 'We should do an emergency pulmonary angiography so that we can find out exactly where the clot is.'

'That's what I thought.'

Matthew supervised the procedure as soon as they had the results of the X-ray and the ECG. They injected a contrast medium into Eve's suspect blood vessel through a fine catheter and watched the recording of the blood flow on a monitor.

'That's a large embolus,' Matthew said quietly. 'No wonder she's in trouble. You'd better put her on thrombolytic drugs to help dissolve the clot, and then refer her urgently for surgery. Notify the intensive care unit as well. With any luck, we'll have caught this in time.'

It was more than two hours later before the rush of patients slowed enough for Sarah to catch her breath again. She leaned against the desk and sipped coffee from a polystyrene cup that she had fetched from the machine.

'You must be desperate to be drinking that stuff,' Matthew commented as he walked by. 'Go and take a proper break in the doctors' lounge.'

'I don't have time. There's another patient coming in—a suspected heart attack.'

'Dr Massey will see to him. You need to sit down before you fall down.'

She shook her head. 'No, I can manage.'

'You won't.' Matthew gave her a stern look. 'That was an order. Go and take a break right now or I shall send you home. You're no good to the department if you work until you collapse. You don't have to prove anything.'

'I wasn't trying to.'

'You could have fooled me.' He considered her thoughtfully. 'I meant what I said the other day… you've been doing too much for too long. You don't have to carry the whole world on your shoulders.'

'I'm just trying to be efficient and to do my best all round. It's important to me that I do the right thing, but I'm not sure that you understand that.'

He grimaced. 'I can see that it's still rankling with you about what I said the other day. I'm sorry about that. You were perfectly right, and it isn't my place to interfere, but I'm concerned about you. For as long as I've known you, you've taken on far too much. It's become a way of life.'

His glance travelled over her. 'You're young, and you should be out there having fun, not worrying about other people all the time. You do enough of that here.'

She smiled wryly at that. 'So do you. What's happened to your social life since you came back here? I thought you would be over at the house nearly every day, but you've hardly been by to see Rachel.'

It bothered her that he was letting her sister down. Perhaps part of Rachel's trouble was that they were making no headway as far as their relationship was concerned. She was a single mother, and likely to stay that way. No one else had come along to sweep her off her feet and perhaps that was because she had no room in her heart for anyone clse but the father of her child.

'She's still away, isn't she?'

'Yes, but I have the feeling that you still wouldn't have gone to visit her. It's almost as though you're deliberately avoiding the house.' She looked at him curiously. 'Has something happened to put you off? You and Rachel always used to get on so well together.'

'That's true, but I'm not sure that it's a good idea to keep in touch just at the moment. Rachel seems to be wary of me these days, and I'm having a problem getting through to her. I want to help her, but now that this trouble has flared up again between my parents and your family, it's going to be doubly difficult. I don't want to upset her or your father. It's bad enough that my parents are being cool towards them.'

'Are you saying that you're sympathetic to Rachel and my dad?'

He sighed. 'I don't want to take sides. It can never be a good situation when two families are at war. I'm caught up in the middle of it, and that doesn't feel right. I've tried talking things through with my parents, but it doesn't make a whole lot of difference. They felt that they were somehow betrayed, and now that Morgan may be back on the scene they want to see some kind of closure. I'm not sure that they're going to get that.'

'I think we'd all like to see it happen. Until it does, we just have to get on with things the best way we can.' She was pensive for a moment. Was that why he and Rachel couldn't get together, because his parents were getting in the way? Wasn't that what Rachel had implied to her father?

In part, she could understand Matthew's difficulty. If he chose to, he could lay his feelings on the line and make it clear that he wanted Rachel, but it wouldn't be easy to reconcile that with his parents or Rachel. They would always be a thorn in the relationship.

He sent her a sideways glance. 'Is that what you're doing—getting on with things the best way you can? You've been caught up in all this the same way that I have, and I know that's part of your problem. You feel that you have to take some of the burden from your father and your sister. Your father's health's deteriorating because of all the stress he's been through, and Rachel has troubles of her own to contend with. Having a child is a tremendous responsibility, and she doesn't seem prepared to share it.'

He was silent for a moment, deep in thought, but then, as though he'd brushed whatever was troubling him to one side, he said, 'How are you coping? Are you finding it difficult, looking after Emily? I know children can be hard work, especially young ones.'

'Emily's a lovely child. So full of energy.' Sarah

laughed. 'Too much sometimes. She's been staying at my cottage these last few nights because I wanted to give my dad a break, but it's hard to know how to keep her amused. She brought quite a lot of her toys over with her, but I feel she needs to get out and about more. The trouble is, my garden's pocket-sized.'

'Perhaps I could help?'

Matthew's offer puzzled her. 'I'm not sure how…'

'She enjoyed playing with Nicky when we went to the fair. Perhaps we could go somewhere together again? The dog's due to go and have his stitches out at the weekend, so I agreed that I would look after Nicky again. We could go to the beach if the weather's fine. It shouldn't take more than half an hour to get to the coast. I'd like the chance to get to know Emily better.'

Sarah thought about it. Did he feel that Rachel was shutting him out? If so, perhaps this would be an ideal opportunity to try to put things right. Rachel was due to come home at the weekend, but not until Saturday evening, and he could use the time to get to know the child.

She decided to go along with the idea. It couldn't do any harm, and in the end it might do some good because Rachel might realise that he wanted to be part of their lives. It might be a way of bringing Rachel and Matthew together again. She wasn't happy to be the one to do it, but they couldn't go on like this.

'All right. I think they would enjoy that.' She drank the last of her coffee and grimaced. 'You're right about that stuff. It's awful.'

He laughed. 'We only drink it for the caffeine.'

'I meant to ask you about the dog, Toby. How is he?'

'He's doing all right. He was very woozy after the anaesthetic, and it took a while for him to get back on his feet, but he seems to be on form again now. The tumour was benign, but they had to remove the spleen for fear of dangerous haemorrhaging. He's not that old, so his other organs should take over in time.'

'That's good. I'm glad it turned out all right.'

An ambulance siren sounded in the distance, and Matthew straightened up, ready for action once more. 'Go and get your break. I'll deal with this one with Dr Massey.'

He called for her at her cottage on Saturday, as they had arranged. Nicky was excited to see Emily again, and the two children chattered non-stop and rampaged about in Sarah's small garden for a while.

'You were right when you described this garden.' Matthew laughed, looking around at the small patch of lawn and the minuscule flowerbeds. 'It certainly is tiny.'

'But perfectly maintained, you have to admit,' she said wryly.

He nodded. 'Seriously, though, you have made the most of it. I like the way you've planted clematis along the back fence. It's very colourful. I take it that was your idea...they weren't here already when you moved in? I know you were always very fond of them.'

'I did put them in, you're right.' She was amazed that he had remembered something like that. 'It's been what you might call a challenge, to make something of this small space, but I'm pleased with it so far. It was a wilderness of weeds when I took it over, but I had a vision of banks of flowers to draw the eye.'

'And you've succeeded in that. It's very colourful.' He smiled. 'You were always busy in your father's garden, weren't you? I remember calling round at the house one day to drop something off for your father and I found you out in the garden on your knees. You were digging up the earth, ready to put in some bedding plants.'

His mouth twisted. 'You were a grimy urchin, with streaks of dirt on your cheeks where you'd been rubbing them with the back of your hand. I remember you looking up at me and squinting because the sun was in your eyes. You had your hair pinned back in some kind of band to keep it out of the way of your face, but most of the curls had worked loose and you kept having to push them back.'

Sarah's cheeks coloured. 'Heavens…that was a long time ago.' She remembered that day all too well. She must have been about eighteen, and she had been mortified because she hadn't been expecting him, and he had come and discovered her in all her mess. She had been wearing blue jeans and a top that had showed her bare midriff. It had ridden up every time she'd leaned forward or lifted her arm, and he had commented that it must have shrunk in the wash. She had felt adolescent and gauche, and she had denied that vigorously. 'It's a crop top,' she had told him, and he had laughed.

She had wished so much that she could have stunned him with her good looks, but in her heart of hearts she had known that it was never going to happen. She hadn't stood a chance of getting a second look when Rachel had been around.

'I'll show you round the house, if you like,' she said now. Calling to the children, she told them that they were going inside.

She led the way to the living room, and Matthew glanced around. 'I like this,' he said. 'The patio doors let in a lot of light.'

She nodded. 'That's one thing that attracted me to this house. It looks small on the outside, but it's bright inside and that makes it seem bigger. It does for me anyway. I would rattle around in anything larger.'

'You didn't think of staying on with your father? It wouldn't make things easier for you, would it?'

'I thought about it, but when Rachel wanted to move back, I thought it might be too much for Dad with both of us living there. Besides, I thought it would be good to be independent.'

'Expensive, too, considering that you had used a lot of your savings to help your father.'

'There was that, but it was worth it to establish myself in my own place. It isn't much but I'm quite proud of it.' She thought about his big house, and asked, 'How are you getting on with the alterations to your place? Have you made a start yet?'

He nodded. 'I've had a builder round to start work on knocking down the wall between the kitchen and utility room, as you suggested. It'll take a while to put things straight, but I think it will be a big improvement. I just need to plan where I want all the cupboard units and fittings and so on.'

'It sounds like a fairly big job to me.' She grinned. 'Perhaps I'm lucky that I don't have that problem here. If I was to knock a wall down, I'd find myself sitting out in the garden.'

She took him on a quick tour of the cottage, and then they came back to the kitchen, where she said, 'Do you think I should pack some lunch to take with us? It wouldn't take more than a few minutes.'

He shook his head. 'There's no need to go to that trouble. I'm sure we'll find a café. I doubt Nicky will eat much anyway. He's been off his food just lately.'

'More tummy problems?'

He nodded. 'He doesn't seem too bad today, but I'll keep an eye on him all the same.'

They bundled the children into the car a short time later. They were excitable, giggling and noisy in the back of the car, but Matthew was good-humoured and tolerant throughout the journey to the coast.

'Here we are,' he announced eventually. He parked the car on the seafront, and they all tumbled out and headed towards the beach.

He'd had the forethought to bring buckets and spades, and they spent the next half-hour or so helping the children to build a huge castle and moat out of sand. Then it became a competition to see who could dig out the best river and make it flow into the sea.

Emily sang as she worked, happy to follow Nicky's lead in whatever he did.

'I'm going to make dinosaur,' Nicky announced, and Emily frowned, not entirely sure what that was, and then set to, piling up sand enthusiastically. They added shells for eyes and teeth, and when it was finished, Sarah solemnly pronounced that it was awesome.

'Gruesome more like...look at those teeth.' Matthew chuckled. 'I'll bet he hasn't seen a dentist in ages.'

Sarah thumped his arm in mock annoyance. 'Don't make fun of our monster. He might be sensitive.'

By lunchtime the sun was fiercely hot, and Matthew hired a sunshade to protect the children from its rays.

'You can go and cool down in the pools left by the sea,' Sarah told them. 'We'll watch you from here.'

They didn't need to be told twice but ran off, whooping and squealing, each child racing to be the one to get there first.

Matthew shielded his eyes from the sun and watched them go. 'I'll go and get us a tray of food from the beach café,' he murmured. 'Is there anything you want in particular? Sandwiches, gooey cake?'

'Nothing special,' she said. 'Whatever you choose will be fine, but perhaps ice cream would help to cool us down.'

'OK. I won't be more than a few minutes.'

The children came back after a while, and she dried them and covered them with more sun block. By the time Matthew returned, they were settled under the shade, ready for their lunch.

Nicky hardly ate anything, as Matthew had expected, and Sarah noticed that the child rubbed his tummy once or twice. He didn't complain, though, and soon after Emily had finished eating the children raced off again towards a nearby hollow in the sand that had filled with sea water.

'Don't you two go off any further away than that,' Matthew said.

All the same, Sarah kept a watchful eye on them.

She bit into her salad sandwich and said, 'Mmm...this is really good. I didn't realise that I was so hungry.'

Matthew watched her finish it off. 'Do you want some more?'

She shook her head. 'No, thanks. That was delicious.' She rubbed her hands together to shake off the crumbs.

'I can tell that you enjoyed it.' He reached up and gently brushed her mouth with his thumb. 'You missed a bit.' He smiled at her, looking into her eyes. 'There, that's better.'

She couldn't speak for a moment, but just stared at him, transfixed by his blue gaze. Her lips were tingling where he had touched her, and her pulse was racing out of control, and to her shame she desperately wanted him to touch her again.

She yearned for it so much that she almost leaned

towards him, and perhaps she had done, or maybe he had read her mind, because he bent his head towards her and the next moment his mouth came down on hers and their lips met and clung together.

Her head was swimming, dizzy with sensation, and she couldn't think straight. All she could think about was this moment in time, the way his kiss deepened, as though he was tasting her, exploring the fullness of her lips. She wanted it to go on and on for ever.

'Uncle Matthew, you said you would take me to the sea and help me fill my bucket with water.'

They drew apart. Sarah felt guilty, as though she had done something wrong, but for the moment she wasn't sure what it was, and Matthew looked perplexed, as though he had forgotten where they were.

Nicky was oblivious to what was going on. He was searching for his bucket. 'Uncle Matthew?' he repeated. 'You take me down there now?'

'Of course. I promised, didn't I?' Matthew stood up in one fluid movement. He glanced at Sarah, but his expression was unreadable, and she looked away. Perhaps, if she pretended that it hadn't happened, all these confused feelings would go away.

It was the sun, that was what had done it… It was hot, far too hot, and she must be suffering from some kind of heatstroke that had left her thoroughly disorientated. That must be the explanation, surely? How else could she have betrayed her sister in such a way?

'Me come,' Emily insisted, scrabbling to her feet. 'Me want fill bucket.'

'That's all right, you can come with us,' Matthew

said. 'We'll get some water to fill the moat up again, shall we?'

Sarah would have gone with them, but she had been shaken to the core by what had just happened and she needed to get her sense of balance back.

They took longer than she had expected, and she was glad of that. It gave her time to put things into perspective. Nothing had really happened, had it? It had just been a kiss, exchanged in the heat of the moment. It had been a temporary aberration, nothing more, and perhaps Matthew had simply been carried away by the way she had looked at him. Had he recognised all that pent-up longing that had impelled her towards him?

Just thinking about it made her burn with shame. She had behaved so badly.

Matthew seemed to have forgotten it anyway. He was perfectly normal in his manner when he came back with the children, and Sarah felt an overwhelming sense of relief.

'I think this bucket leaks,' he said with a laugh. 'Either that or Emily's walking with a wobble. It started off full to the brim, and now there's hardly any water left in it.'

Emily gave him an old-fashioned look. She put her hands on her hips and said, 'You was 'posed to be carrying it.'

He ruffled her curls. 'I guess I'll have to go and fill it up all over again, won't I?'

All four of them trekked down to the water's edge this time. They brought back enough water to satisfy the children, and then Matthew and Sarah sat down and looked on while Emily covered Nicky's legs with wet sand. The boy looked a little pale, Sarah thought.

'Emily's her mother all over, isn't she?' Matthew murmured. 'So dainty and full of fun. She was singing all the pop songs just a while ago, with not a care in the world.' He gave a faint smile. 'Rachel used to do that when she worked at her sewing machine. She said it helped her to concentrate.'

'She still does sometimes.' Except that lately she had been preoccupied. She had things on her mind, and Sarah wondered if her holiday would have helped her to sort things out.

She glanced at Matthew, but he was deep in thought. After a while, he said, 'Have you ever thought about having a child of your own?'

'I've thought about it, yes.'

'And?'

'I suppose the right man would have to come along.' She was wistful for a moment, thinking about that. The only man she had ever considered as a father for her children was sitting right next to her, but he wasn't applying for the situation, was he?

She got to her feet. 'I think it's time we were making a move for home,' she said briskly. 'Rachel will be back soon, and she'll want to see Emily.'

'Right.' He stood up and brushed the sand off his trousers. 'Let's get things organised.'

They prepared for the journey home, and neither of them mentioned the kiss. It was as though it had never happened.

CHAPTER SEVEN

MATTHEW halted his car outside Sarah's father's house and frowned. There was another vehicle parked on the drive, a sleek, top-of-the-range BMW, and he looked it over and said, 'That's my parents' car. I wonder what they're doing here?'

'I was just wondering the same thing,' Sarah murmured. 'I don't think they've been here in years. Not since the trouble with my father's business anyway.'

She was worried. They could only be here to talk about the fact that Casey Morgan had been found, and that wasn't good news. Raking up the past was bound to be upsetting for her father.

'Is my mummy home?' Emily piped up from the back seat.

'I don't think so, not yet. I expect she'll be here in a little while.' Sarah glanced at the children. If Matthew's parents were around, it might be a good idea to keep the children occupied while they talked. 'You two could go and play in Emily's room for a while,' she told them. 'You could show Nicky your box of dressing-up things,' she suggested to Emily.

The little girl nodded. 'I will.'

They went into the house, and the children raced upstairs. Walking along the hallway, Sarah could hear the sound of a heated discussion coming from the living room. She winced, pausing outside the door. She didn't have a good feeling about any of this.

Matthew followed her into the room.

'I don't understand what your problem is,' his father was saying. 'Morgan's back in the country, but you're still debating what to do about the situation. As far as I'm concerned, there isn't any question at all. He should be prosecuted, and you should be making sure that the case goes ahead.'

'I've heard that the man is ill. He probably won't be able to stand trial,' her father said. 'I feel as badly as you do about what happened, but I don't see that we're going to get anywhere by pursuing this in the long run.'

Stephen Bayford clearly didn't agree. His mouth made a tight line. 'I don't believe he's as ill as he makes out. He's pulled the wool over your eyes once before and he's doing it again now. Just like last time, you're letting him get away with it.'

Sarah walked further into the room. 'Mr Bayford…don't you think you're being a little unreasonable? This has all happened very recently, and none of us know all the details yet. We have to rely on what we know at the moment and that is that the man needs hospital treatment. You're not being fair to my father by harassing him this way.'

'I have a right to see justice done,' he bit back, and Sarah almost flinched at his harsh tone. He looked every bit the successful businessman, and she guessed he wasn't used to having his plans thwarted.

He was tall, smartly dressed in a dark, expensively

tailored suit, even though it was the weekend, and she wondered if he was going to keep an appointment after this visit or if he was planning on going somewhere special.

Somewhere special, she decided on balance. He looked like a man who had every aspect of his life planned out, and it was hardly surprising that the shocking outcome of his business venture with her father still infuriated him. She didn't think that anyone would ever easily have got the better of him and it must stick in his throat that Morgan might get away with what he had done.

'We all want to see justice done,' her father said. He was very pale, and Sarah could hear the rasp of his lungs as he struggled for breath. She was worried that he might be in pain.

Her father added, 'Don't you realise that by dredging all this up again, the story could end up in the newspapers, just as it did before? I'm not sure that would do any of us any good.'

Matthew's mother interrupted. She, too, was elegantly dressed in a tapered skirt and plain top beneath a fitted jacket. Her hair was a glossy chestnut colour, cut in a chic style that made the most of her features. 'We know very well what it means to have our picture splashed all over the newspapers,' she said. 'We were innocent victims, but that didn't make any difference. The journalists made out that we were taken for a ride. We were made to look foolish, and it's time that man paid for what he did.'

'I don't think any of us will come out of this feeling

better,' Sarah's father said. 'My business suffered because of what he did, and it wasn't helped by the press coverage. I think the same thing will happen again. You think that you're going to be vindicated, but stories sometimes get twisted when they go to print, and it hardly ever turns out the way that you expect. I know finding Morgan and pressing charges was the plan all along, but now I'm not so sure. If we persist and take him to court, we'll be hounding a man who is at death's door. I, for one, don't want that on my conscience.'

'Then you're a fool.' Stephen glowered at James. 'He was ill when he came over here, I grant you, and he was in hospital for a time, but they've let him go home. They say he needs to be with his family for his last few weeks, but it's all a sham, if you ask me. I don't believe a word of it. He lied to you once before and he'll lie again to get himself out of a tight corner. If you take his word for anything, you deserve to go under.'

Matthew decided to intervene. 'Dad, I think you should let things cool down for a bit. Why don't you and Mum give James more time to think things through? As Sarah says, Morgan's only just come back to the country. Nothing's going to happen for a while. The lawyers need to work on it.'

'Lawyers…' His father almost spat the word out. 'Let them get to work on this and all they'll do is line their own pockets. They're the ones who've engineered this ''going home to die'' farce.'

Sarah watched her father reach behind him to

steady himself against the arm of a chair. She thought he looked shaky on his feet, and she was concerned for him.

'Stephen, Teresa…I think Matthew's right,' she said. 'You've said what you had to say, and I think you should leave my father now to come to his own decision. He's not well, and you're not helping him.'

It was as though Stephen hadn't heard her. 'He let that man walk all over him once before and now he's letting him do it again…don't you see that?' He was not to be deterred.

'I'm sorry, but I want you to leave now,' Sarah said firmly. 'This discussion's at an end.'

Stephen opened his mouth to object, but Matthew put a hand on his shoulder and gently turned him around. 'Come on, Dad. It's for the best. There's no point in saying any more, and anyway you'll be late for the show.' He turned to his mother. 'It is this evening you're going into town, isn't it?'

His mother nodded.

'I'll see you to the door,' Matthew murmured. 'We can talk about this later.'

Sarah left him to see them out. Her father was ashen-faced and struggling for breath, and she was afraid that he was about to collapse. He was swaying on his feet, and she went over to him and gently helped him down into a chair.

'Are you in pain?' she asked.

'I just feel a bit unsteady, that's all,' he managed. 'Nothing to worry about. Just give me a second or two.'

She shook her head. 'I'm going to get my medical bag. You're not well, and I'm going to examine you and find out what's wrong.'

He didn't argue with her, and that was a bad sign. It meant that he was too ill to put up a fight.

Coming back into the room a moment later, she helped him to undo his shirt, and then she ran her stethoscope over his chest. She listened carefully to the sound of his heart, and then she took his pulse and his blood pressure.

'Your GP gave you digoxin, didn't he? When did you last take it?'

'A couple of hours ago.'

'It's not controlling your heart rate enough at the moment,' she said softly. 'I can give you an injection of something that will help to settle things down.'

He nodded, and she went ahead and gave him the injection. 'Your lungs are very congested,' she told him, 'and I think this is all part of the same problem. We really need to talk about your health, you know. We need to sort out what we can do to get you properly back on your feet…not right now, but in a little while when you're feeling a bit better. Sit still and rest.'

She stayed quietly by his side until it looked as though the injection was taking effect, and then she ran her stethoscope over his chest once more. 'That's better,' she murmured. 'Do you think you'll be all right if I leave you for a couple of minutes to go and put the kettle on? I think a cup of tea might help.'

'Yes. Things feel a lot calmer now.' He managed a smile. 'A cup of tea would be nice.'

She patted his shoulder. 'I won't be long.'

She walked into the kitchen and saw that Matthew was already there, setting out a tray with cups and teapot. He turned to her, and said, 'How is he?'

'Steadier, I think. His heart rhythm was chaotic for a while.' She paused, trying to calm herself. At work she could cope reasonably well, but this was her father who was suffering, and the last few minutes had been upsetting. 'I was afraid for him.'

'I could see that. I saw that you were treating him and I didn't want to disturb you. What do you think's wrong?'

Sarah said unhappily, 'I suspect one of his heart valves isn't working as it should. He really needs to go to the hospital and get things checked out properly. He's such a stubborn man at times, but I think I'm going to be equally obstinate and insist that he gets specialist help. He can't go on like this.'

She leaned back against the worktop, feeling drained all of a sudden. Her father would have to undergo tests, and she was worried about the outcome of all this.

Watching her, Matthew came over to her and drew her into his arms, comforting her, holding her close, and just then it seemed the most natural thing in the world to be in his embrace, as though that was where she belonged.

'I'm sorry for what happened,' he said softly. 'I don't think my parents have any idea how sick he is.

I'm sure my father wouldn't have gone on the way he did if he'd realised.'

'No, probably not.' She wasn't entirely sure that was true, but she wasn't going to argue the point. It was good having Matthew nearby. He was warm and solid, a port of call in a storm, and it was comforting to know that he was there for her. His strength was something tangible, something she could rely on to help her to get through this.

He drew her head down against his chest, and stroked her hair soothingly, his fingers brushing away the strands that fell damply on to her cheeks. She hadn't realised that she was crying, but the tears were trickling slowly down and he brushed them away gently with his thumb.

'I could have a word with Fraser Dunstan if you like. He's a friend of mine, and he's well respected as a cardiac surgeon. If anyone can sort out your father's problem, I'm sure he can.'

She nodded. 'Let me talk to my dad first. I'll see if I can get him to co-operate.'

'Do you want me to talk to him with you? Perhaps I can help you to persuade him that it's a good thing to do.'

'No.' She looked up into his eyes. 'I don't think that would be a good idea right now. He might feel pressurised if we tackle him together, as though we were ganging up on him. I'll think of something. I have to—he can't go on this way. He tries to hide it from me, but I know he's in pain, and I'm afraid because I can see that he's vulnerable.'

She bit her lip. 'It doesn't seem fair that he should be suffering this way. All his life he's worked hard and struggled to make a success of things, and I can't help thinking that he hasn't been dealt a fair hand.'

Her mouth trembled a little, and she made an effort to pull herself together. What was she doing, weeping all over Matthew? She had more backbone than this, didn't she?

His lips brushed her forehead. 'I'm here if you need me. Just remember that you're not on your own in this.'

His kiss was gentle, and soothing on her shattered nerves. She relaxed against him, taking comfort in the peaceful moment, letting his tender concern smooth away her worries. He didn't mean anything by it, except to reassure her, and she shouldn't read anything more into his gesture, but it was good while it lasted.

'I know. Thank you for that.' She straightened up. 'I must get back to him. I need to make sure that he's all right.'

He let her go. 'Of course. You go and see to him. Shall I bring the tea in, or would me being here bring on another attack, do you think?'

'I think it might upset him.' She looked at him with troubled eyes. 'Your family hasn't been doing him much good lately, and I don't want to risk another jolt to his heart. Perhaps it would be for the best if you leave now. I think he's just too frail to stand any more at the moment.'

He nodded, but his expression was grim and she was sure that she must have offended him. He had tried to help her and now she was pushing him away. 'As you like,' he said flatly. 'I'll go and fetch Nicky, and we'll let ourselves out. Shall I send Emily down to you?'

'Yes, if you would, thanks. I'll get her to do some colouring in while I talk to my dad. Rachel should be home soon to take care of her.'

He left the house a few minutes later, and Sarah settled Emily at the table with a colouring book. When she was sure that the child was occupied, she went to sit with her father.

'At least some of the colour's come back into your cheeks,' she said. 'You had me worried there for a while.'

'I'm fine now,' he said on a rueful note. 'I'll have to try not to let things get to me so easily. I shouldn't have got worked up, but Bayford was provoking me and trying to make me go against my better judgement.'

She shook her head. 'It didn't happen just because he was hassling you. You're ill, Dad, and this isn't something that's just going to fade away if you try to ignore it. I think that there's something wrong with one of your heart valves, and that's why you're having these nasty episodes. With the valve not working properly, your heart's having to work extra hard. That's why you're getting pain in your chest, and the discomfort is making you breathless. You have to face up to the fact that you're not going to get any better unless we do something about it.'

'No, it isn't as bad as all that, not really.' He gave

her a weak smile. 'I'll be all right. I'll keep on with the tablets, and I'll stay calm and not let things upset me.'

'That's not going to work,' she told him. 'It's lucky that I was here when your heart started to play up and I was able to do something for you. Another time, things might be much worse. You need to get treatment before things get out of control, and that might mean that you need to have an operation to put things right.'

He shook his head. 'No. I'm sure it won't come to that. I'll be careful and I'll get by without all that fuss and bother.'

She studied his features carefully. 'Why are you so against going to the hospital to get yourself checked out? What is it that's worrying you?'

He grimaced. 'I'm not worried. Anyway, when can I spare the time to go and have tests and perhaps stay in hospital to have things put right? The business isn't going to run itself, is it?'

'If you don't get your health sorted out, the business won't survive anyway because you won't be in a position to work at all,' she told him flatly. 'Anyway, until you have the tests done, we won't know exactly what's involved. As soon as we know what the situation is, and what needs to be done, we'll be better able to work out how we can manage the business.'

She gently squeezed his hand and looked into his eyes. 'You're not just a one-man band anyway, and you have a workforce that you can rely on. If it comes to an operation, I'm sure your secretary can handle day-to-day matters, and it might be possible that we can bring someone in to help out with the more practical side of things. Surely it's better to think ahead and plan for what might happen than to have to undergo a major upheaval because you suddenly collapse. Where would the business be then? You've worked so hard to keep it going, and you can't throw it all away now by burying your head in the sand.'

He gave her a wry smile. 'You're not going to give up on this, are you?'

'No, I'm not. I shan't be happy until I know that you're fit and well. What kind of a person would I be if I let my own father work himself into the ground? It's not going to happen.'

'So, what do you think I should do now?'

'Leave it with me. I've got the name of a good heart surgeon, a Mr Dunstan. I'll ask him if he'll have a look at you, and if he thinks that you need surgery, we'll try to arrange it for a time to suit you, so that you've time to organise what needs to be done where the business is concerned.'

He nodded wearily, giving in. 'All right. You do what you think is best.'

She set the wheels in motion as soon as she went back to work. Matthew was preoccupied and not inclined to chat, but when she approached him about her father he put her in touch with Fraser Dunstan, and told her that he would phone him later to explain the situation.

Mr Dunstan agreed readily enough to see her father, and arranged for him to have an appointment with him in a couple of weeks' time.

Rachel brought their father into hospital on the day of his appointment with the consultant, and stopped by the A and E department for a while.

'Are you busy?' she asked Sarah. 'I thought I would come in and see you while Dad's with Mr Dunstan.'

Sarah shook her head. 'We're fairly quiet here this morning.' She smiled. 'I don't suppose that will last for long.' She took Rachel to the doctors' lounge, and poured coffee for them both from the filter machine. 'Did you have any trouble getting Dad here?'

'It wasn't too bad. He was a bit grumpy first thing, but he didn't give me any real problems. I think he realised it was inevitable that he would need treatment. There have been lots of episodes recently that showed him that he couldn't go on the way he is. He struggles for breath and the slightest effort can bring on his chest pain.'

The door to the lounge opened, and Matthew walked in. 'Hello, Rachel,' he said with a smile. 'I thought I saw you arrive.'

Rachel glanced at him warily. 'I'm not staying. I just came to have a quick word with Sarah.'

'I guessed that. Sarah told me that you were bringing your father to the hospital today.' He looked her over appreciatively. 'You're in great shape. Your holiday must have done you some good…there's more colour in your cheeks and you look revitalised.'

'I feel better,' she agreed. 'I was in two minds

whether to go away at all, but Sarah and my dad
thought it would be a good idea, and I'm glad that I
did now. It's given me a better perspective on things.
Of course, I couldn't have done it without Sarah's
help. If she hadn't looked after Emily for me, it would
have been a non-starter.'

'So where is Emily?'

'They've found her a place at the local nursery
school. She enjoyed going to the crèche so much that
I decided I'd see how she would get on at the place
near to us. It's only a couple of mornings a week,
Tuesdays and Fridays, but so far she's taken to it
really well.'

'Does that mean that you have time on your hands,
or are you doing extra work from home?'

'I've not taken on any more just at the moment. I
need to keep an eye on Dad and I'm just enjoying
having time to myself for a while.'

He nodded. 'Perhaps we could meet for coffee one
day when she's at nursery school? When I'm on the
later shift, maybe? We haven't really had the chance
to get together and talk properly, have we, with me
working and you going to the coast?' He studied her
features carefully, and she looked away.

'That's true. I've had a few things on my mind
lately, and I needed a break.' She drew in a deep
breath, and then said cautiously, 'You could be right,
though. It might be a good idea for us to talk things
through.'

'Good. We'll make that a date, then, shall we? How
about meeting me on Friday morning?'

Rachel swallowed. 'Friday…yes. That would be fine.'

They talked for a while longer about this and that, and Sarah joined in occasionally. Rachel and Matthew were getting along better than they had done for a while, and she told herself that she was pleased for her sister.

It bothered her, though, that only a couple of weeks ago she had been in Matthew's arms and he had been holding her and kissing her and making her dream of what might be, and now he was chatting up Rachel, and there was every possibility that their relationship might be taking off once more. Would it last?

Whichever way it went, the only certain thing was that Sarah would be left out in the cold once again. Matthew would go back to being like a brother to her and, if she was honest with herself, that was how it should be, that was how it had always been.

It was confusing, and it was upsetting and, try as she may, she didn't know what she should do to make the sick feeling in her stomach go away.

CHAPTER EIGHT

'WHY is Mrs Jackson still waiting around?' Matthew was frowning as he walked towards Sarah. She was just finishing a phone call to the laboratory, and now she put the receiver down and looked up at him.

'I'm still waiting for a bed for her.'

'Then you'd better chase things up and get things moving. We've more patients coming in and we need to clear the backlog.'

She sent him a mystified look. 'I'm doing my best.'

It wasn't like Matthew to pressurise his staff, and she didn't understand why his manner had changed so much this last week or so. It was as though nothing mattered but the work in hand. He had been distant and almost unapproachable, at least as far as she was concerned.

'Is something wrong?' she asked. 'I mean, other than at work? You don't seem to have been your usual self lately. I don't seem to be able to talk to you these days as I used to.' At the back of her mind, she wondered if his relationship with Rachel wasn't going as smoothly as he would have liked.

He was busy signing a chart, but he lifted his head and glanced at her now. 'Nothing's wrong. Why should it be?'

She gave a negligent shrug. 'I know that you saw

Rachel the other day, and she seemed very subdued when she came home. I wondered if things had gone wrong between the two of you.'

'It was no more than I expected. I'm trying to make some headway with her, but Rachel will never be herself while this business is going on between your father and Morgan. She's worried about whether there'll be a trial, and she thinks that if my parents don't back off, your father's illness will be made worse. There's nothing I can do except to talk to my parents and ask them to ease off. With the best will in the world, I can't change what happened, and when all's said and done they have a justifiable grievance.'

'My father's trying to put that right.'

'I know he is. In the meantime, he's making himself ill with worry, according to Rachel.' His mouth made a straight line. 'What happened at his meeting with Dunstan? Rachel wasn't too sure about the results. Did the tests confirm what you thought?'

She nodded. 'He said that one of Dad's heart valves is narrowed, and that's the reason he's having all his problems. He wants to operate, but my dad's worried about taking time off from the business. I'm trying to get him to see sense, but it's an uphill task.'

'That's your father all over, isn't it? He can be as stubborn as a mule at times.' He pushed the chart back into its slot in the box just as an ambulance siren sounded in the distance. 'We should get on,' he muttered. 'There are patients waiting.'

He was back to his businesslike self once more,

and Sarah sighed inwardly and went to see what she could do about finding Mrs Jackson a bed.

The next few hours were hectic as they dealt with the aftermath of a road traffic accident. There were open fractures and chest injuries, and they were so busy dealing with everyone who came in that there was little time for talk.

By mid-afternoon things had quietened down, and Sarah was hoping for the chance to grab a quick coffee. Before she was able to do that, though, the paramedics brought in a man who was in a desperate condition. He was being given oxygen, and the paramedic believed that there was some intestinal bleeding.

'His son called the ambulance,' the paramedic told Sarah. 'He said his father was being treated for liver problems and his condition was deteriorating fast. He's semi-conscious.'

'OK. Thanks. I'll handle things from here.' Sarah moved forward to assess the man on the trolley, and then stood back, shocked to the core. She recognised him, and for a moment she hesitated, unable to bring herself to do anything to help him.

Helen, the nurse assisting, suggested quietly, 'Should we take him through to bay three?'

Sarah didn't answer. She ought to be examining the man, doing what she could to save his life, but it was as though she had been turned to stone. Vaguely, she was aware of Helen summoning Matthew, and a moment later he came to stand by her side.

'What's the problem here?'

Helen said softly, 'Mr Morgan has symptoms of liver failure. The paramedics suspect that there's a degree of cerebral oedema. Shall I start him on mannitol?'

'We'll decide that in a moment. In the meantime, it might help to raise him up a little so that his head's at 45 degrees.' He turned to Sarah and said sharply, 'This man needs attention now. Do you want me to take over?'

Sarah jerked, pulled up by his tone. 'No. I'll see to him.'

His eyes narrowed on her. 'Are you sure you're up to it? He's a patient like any other, and you shouldn't let your feelings get in the way. If you think you can't cope, you should stand back.'

'I can manage.' She took in a deep breath and walked to the treatment bay.

She examined Casey Morgan, but all the time she felt as though she was working like an automaton. This was the man who had caused her father so much stress, who had brought so much heartache to her family by milking the business of funds and destroying everything her father had worked for. It took everything she had in her to treat him with the care and compassion her profession demanded of her.

'I'm going to put in a nasogastric tube,' she told Helen. 'Would you take blood for blood glucose, prothrombin, urea and electrolytes, and liver-function tests, then we'll do an EEG.'

She was conscious that Matthew was still by her side. He was watching proceedings, and she didn't blame him for doubting that she would take proper care of her patient. She had hesitated, but now she was doing what needed to be done.

She put in the tube, and told Helen, 'I'm going to give him sucralfate to minimise the gastro-intestinal haemorrhaging. He'll need potassium supplements, and amoxycillin to combat sepsis. When we get the results of the blood tests, he may need a platelet infusion, and if he's hypoglycaemic we'll give him dextrose intravenously. We'll give 100 mils of 20 per cent mannitol and monitor the intracranial pressure. I'm setting up an intravenous infusion of dopamine, but we'll need to keep an eye on his fluid balance.'

Matthew intervened. 'You should be aware of the possibility of renal failure,' he said.

Sarah nodded. 'I'm aware of that. At the level of dopamine I'm using, it shouldn't be a problem.'

He nodded. 'OK. You seem to have everything under control here. His son is probably wondering what happened to him. Do you want me to go and talk to him?'

She had forgotten about the son. 'No, I'll do it. Where is he?'

'Helen said that she'd sent him to the relatives' room.'

'I'll go and see him now.' She turned and walked out into the corridor.

It was some years since she had seen Robert Morgan, and she had only fleetingly known him, but he had strong features, and she recognised him instantly. He hadn't changed much, except that he looked troubled, and there were faint lines around his eyes that she had ever noticed before.

He looked up as she went into the room. 'Sarah, it's you...I hadn't expected...' He stared at the name badge she wore on her cotton top. 'I didn't know you were a doctor.'

'It's a small world, isn't it? I hadn't expected that we would meet again either.'

A small crooked line indented his brow. 'Have you been looking after my father?'

'I have.'

'How is he?'

She chose her words carefully. 'I think you know that his condition is very serious. We're doing what we can for him to support him through this phase, but I'm afraid that his liver has been damaged too much, and it has begun to fail. The outlook isn't good.'

His features were pale. 'The doctors who have been treating him say he doesn't have long, perhaps weeks or maybe months at most.'

'I think I would agree with that.'

'Is he in pain?'

'I don't believe so.'

Robert began to pace the floor. 'I know this must be as difficult for you as it is for me,' he said. 'I know how you feel about my father.'

'Would you prefer it if somebody else treated him?'

He looked surprised at that. Perhaps he hadn't expected her to give him the choice. He shook his head. 'No. I'm sure you're doing the best you can.'

He paused, and she wondered if he was thinking how he should frame his words. Then he said, 'I'm sorry for the way my father behaved towards your family. He was deeply in debt, and he felt as though he was being hounded from all sides. He didn't know which way to turn.'

Sarah's mouth tightened. 'Is that supposed to justify what he did? My father depended on him as a partner for his expertise and his support but, instead of helping him, he robbed him and left him to deal with the mess.'

'I know that. I wasn't trying to excuse him…I was just trying to explain. I hoped you might understand.'

'No, I don't understand, and you're wasting your time trying to explain his actions to me. There's only one thing I know for a fact and that's that he ruined my father's life. I'll never forgive him for that.'

The door creaked, and they both turned to see Matthew come into the room. He looked from one to the other, and must have gauged the level of tension sparking between them.

'I came to say that your father is comfortable now,' he said quietly, looking at Robert. 'We're going to admit him, so that he can be given supportive therapy for a while.'

Robert nodded. 'Thank you. I appreciate what you're doing for him.' He grimaced. 'I know that you probably think he doesn't deserve to be treated well after what he did, but I am grateful to you for helping him now. He's my father and I love him despite his faults. He behaved badly, and I wish there was some way I could make amends, but I don't know how.'

'Words come easily,' Sarah said. 'I love my father, too, but he's ill because of all the stress that your father put him through, and I don't know what to do about that either. He's going to have to come into hospital for treatment, and his business will probably fall apart as a result. He'll be back to square one.'

'Sarah…' Matthew put a hand lightly on her shoulder. 'I know you're upset, but this won't help matters.'

To Robert, he said, 'Your father deserves the same care as any patient who comes here. It's not our place to make judgements.'

Robert was frowning. 'I know that it's not easy for you,' he said, looking at Sarah. 'It wasn't just words…I meant what I said. If there's any way I can help out, then I'm prepared to do it. I've been out of the country for the last few years—not with my father. I've been working to improve my qualifications. You perhaps don't realise it, but I worked for your father for a time, and if there's anything I can do to help keep his business afloat, I'm willing to do it. Perhaps I could help out while he's in hospital?'

'No,' Sarah said heatedly. 'I won't hear of you going anywhere near the business. Your father's done enough damage already, and I'm not going to give you the opportunity to do any more.'

'I promise you, you can trust me. I know that it sounds impossible, but I do want to make amends, believe me.' His brow furrowed. 'Perhaps I would do better talking to your father about it.'

Sarah's green eyes flashed at that. 'You stay away from my family,' she said through tight lips. 'I won't have you going anywhere near them.'

Suddenly she couldn't take it any more, and she turned away and rushed out of the room and down the corridor towards the glass doors that led to the back of the hospital. She heard Matthew call after her, but she didn't stop. Suddenly she couldn't breathe and she was frantic to get some air.

Outside, she found a quiet, walled area of landscaped garden where there was a patch of grass and trees and clean air, and she leaned back against the brick wall and pulled ragged gulps of oxygen into her lungs.

Matthew found her there a few minutes later, and she sent him a warning glare. 'Have you come to tell me that I was wrong? I know what you're going to say. He's a relative of somebody who's ill and I should never have spoken to him like that. I know how it should be, but I'm not a saint. I can't pretend that everything's all right, because it isn't.'

'Sarah, I know you're distressed. It was difficult for you back there, I know that.' He reached for her, his hands cupping her shoulders. 'You're assuming that Robert is like his father, but he may not be like that at all. He's offering to help out, to make up for what his father did, and I think you should listen to him. He wants to work with your father again and that might be a solution. Perhaps you should give him a chance.'

'I won't. How can you even ask me such a thing?' Her vision was blurred with tears as she looked up at him. 'Don't you care about what happened before? Don't you realise that the same thing could happen again? I'm not going to make the mistake my father did.'

'It doesn't have to be that way. You could put safe-guards in place. Deny him access to any of the bank accounts. Make sure that somebody is there to super-vise him. There are ways that you can allow him to help.'

She shook her head. 'I won't do it. Just the fact that he is around could tip my father over the edge. I can't come to terms with the fact that you're even suggesting it.'

'You're overwrought, and you're not thinking straight.' His hands moved up to caress her cheeks, and he looked down into her eyes with compassion and understanding. 'I wouldn't do anything to hurt you for the world, surely you know that? I'm only saying that you shouldn't close your mind to what he's suggesting.'

'I'm not going to listen to what you have to say. You and your parents have never understood what it's been like for us. We've been through hell and back and all you ever did was tell us where we went wrong. I don't want to hear it any more. Leave me alone.'

'I'm not going to leave you. It wasn't like that, Sarah. I don't want to see you upset like this. I know things have been difficult for you with my family, but it doesn't have to be that way. I need you to know that I'm here for you. I want to help you if only you would let me. If I could just make you understand...'

He drew her to him. 'Let me show you...'

His lips came down on hers, gentle at first, exploring the softness of her mouth as though he would soothe all her troubles away. She was too startled to resist, too taken up in the powerful surge of her emotions to even think of pulling away.

Then he moved in closer and deepened the kiss, and she lost the will to fight him. His hands stroked along her spine, smoothing over the curve of her hips and tracing the soft contours of her body with ever-increasing boldness.

The touch of his hands was like a balm to her wounded senses. It was as though she had been on a battleground and now he was calming her, massaging away the knot of pain that tormented her. His body moulded itself to hers, and she clung to him, needing him, wanting more, and as his hands became more daring, he fanned the flames of all the passion that was in her soul. The blood sizzled in her veins, and she longed to feel his warm kisses on her bare flesh. She trembled against him, and her body was weak with desire.

'Sarah,' he murmured, 'you have to believe me...I want you to be happy. I want to take away all the hurt and unhappiness. Let me help you.'

'No, I can't.'

She wanted to believe him, but at the back of her

mind something was telling her that this wasn't real. He was kissing her as though he cared for her, but the fact that she was in his arms wasn't going to change anything. He didn't even understand her way of thinking. She was the only one who could make the problem go away. She had to be strong enough to protect her father, and to ensure that Rachel and Emily could find happiness.

Shakily, she tried to draw away from him, but he only held onto her more firmly.

She began to struggle. Wasn't she letting her sister down by being here with him this way?

'This is wrong,' she muttered. 'This is all wrong. I can't let you do this.'

'Sarah—'

She was already turning away from him. 'I have to get back to work.' She didn't look back, but hurried along the path back to A and E.

Why had he kissed her that way? Didn't he have any loyalty to Rachel?

Perhaps he had never loved Rachel, and that was why things were still not settled between them. Whatever the outcome was to be, it was a terrible situation and somebody was bound to get hurt.

CHAPTER NINE

'Why is Rachel in such a hurry?' Sarah said to her father with a frown. 'She's hardly said a word to either of us and now she's off out somewhere. Is she all right, do you think? She looks distracted.' She was kneeling down, tending to the weeds in the flower borders at her father's house, but now she stopped, leaning back on her haunches to watch her sister disappear into the house.

'There's no use asking me what it's all about,' her father said. 'I've never really understood what makes women tick. All I know is that she had a phone call just before you came, and now she's rushing off some place or other.'

He was sitting out in the garden, glancing through his newspaper, but now he put the paper to one side and appeared to be thinking hard. 'Come to think of it, she may have mentioned Matthew's name. Yes, in fact, she did. She said she was going out with him for lunch. And there's Emily, of course. She's at a birthday party, and Rachel said something about picking her up at five o'clock. I imagine she'll do that on her way back.'

So Matthew had called and Rachel was rushing off to meet him. That only made Sarah feel all the more wretched for what had happened the other day. She was still consumed with guilt for the way she had responded to his kiss, and she felt doubly upset for the way she was deceiving her sister.

'It's good of you to come and do the garden for me,' her father said, bringing her out of her reverie. 'I know how busy you are. It has been getting too much for me lately, and it was frustrating not being able to tackle it properly. I really don't know where I'd be without you two girls.'

'You know that we're glad to help, Dad.'

'Yes, and I appreciate it. At least my work isn't too physical, and I can more or less cope with that. Perhaps after I've had this operation I'll be able to do a lot more.'

He was frowning, looking worried, and Sarah asked, 'Is something troubling you? Are you worried about the operation?'

'I think it's more that I don't really know what's involved, or even how the problem came about. The surgeon did explain things to me, but you know how it is—you tend not to take everything in. It's hospitals, I suppose. They can make people nervous.'

'I can explain it to you, if you like.' He nodded and she quickly put down her trowel and pulled off her gardening gloves, laying them down on the lawn. Then she went and sat down next to him at the table on the patio.

'What's happened is that a heart valve has narrowed, and that means your blood struggles to get around your body, and your heart has to work harder.

That's the reason that you get your chest pain, and it's also causing your lungs to become congested.'

Her father looked puzzled. 'But why has this heart valve become narrowed? I try to watch my diet and make sure that I'm eating the right things.'

'We can't be sure. Usually the damage is caused by a rheumatic illness, but sometimes there may be no medical record to show that you've had that kind of episode. Perhaps you were ill at some time, but didn't have any treatment.'

He was frowning. 'I wasn't well when your mother died. I put it down to all the worry and upset at the time, but I suppose it could have been something more. After she was involved in that accident, I was left with you two young girls to bring up, and I suppose I neglected my health a bit.'

'That could be it. The valve would have been damaged, and recently things have been getting worse, so that your heart has been beating chaotically.'

'So what is the surgeon going to do to put it right?'

'Mr Dunstan says that he's going to do what they call a balloon valvuloplasty. It's a fairly new technique that has been developed so that in some cases people don't have to undergo invasive surgery. It will widen the valve so that it functions better. You'll be given a local anaesthetic, and then he'll make a small incision in an artery or vein so that he can put in a catheter. He'll pass the tube along the blood vessel and into the heart, and then he'll inflate the balloon to widen the valve.'

She glanced at him and saw that he was grimacing.

She smiled. 'It might be a little uncomfortable, but it won't be too bad, I promise. The great thing about it is that you won't have to have your chest opened up, and so your recovery should be easier.'

'That's true. I hadn't thought of it that way. How long will I be out of action?'

'You'll be in hospital for a couple of days, I should imagine. After that, you should recover at home for a time and we'll have to wait and see how well you cope. It may take a while for your lungs to clear.'

'So I'll still need to find some way to keep the business going.'

'We'll think of something. It may be that we can get someone with managerial experience to take over temporarily. You've a good, loyal workforce and, from what you've told me, the majority of the men are competent enough to carry on with their own particular projects without supervision. Your secretary can perhaps keep other things on hold for a while.'

He didn't appear to be convinced. 'I don't know...some of the jobs we're working on are urgent. They need to be completed on time. Business is just beginning to pick up and we can't afford to let things slide.'

'The last thing you need to do is to worry. Concentrate on getting your health back. That's the important thing.'

When Rachel came back later that day, she made no mention of her meeting with Matthew. She was quiet, seemingly preoccupied with her own thoughts, and on a couple of occasions when Sarah spoke to her she appeared not to have heard her.

Even so, Sarah persisted. 'We need to try to think of a way to help Dad cope with the business while he's in hospital,' she said. 'It's worrying him, and I wondered if we could contact a specialist agency to find an engineer who could take over for a while.'

'I know. It's been worrying me, too. We'll have to think of something.' Rachel busied herself, clearing up Emily's toys that were lying around. Then she said, 'I need to go and find out what Emily's up to. I can hear her banging around upstairs.'

Sarah frowned. There was no point in trying to talk to Rachel about the problems with the business, was there? She had tried and got nowhere. Perhaps Rachel was too taken up with worrying about her relationship with Matthew to concentrate on anything else.

Sarah went to work in A and E a couple of days later, wondering if she could talk to Matthew about what was going on. Rachel wouldn't thank her for interfering, but events over these last few weeks had been playing on her mind, and she wanted them settled once and for all. It wasn't right that Matthew could kiss Sarah one day and then lead Rachel on.

'He isn't in today,' Helen told her, looking harassed. 'He's giving a talk at a conference in Cornwall. He said he'll be in tomorrow as usual, though. What's the betting something major blows up while he's away?'

'I dare say we'll manage. If anything big crops up, we still have senior staff we can call on.'

She wasn't so sure about that just a few hours later. An ambulance crew brought a child into the department for emergency treatment, and Sarah was horrified to discover that it was little Nicky.

His mother was distraught. Her short chestnut hair was awry where she had been agitatedly pushing it back.

'He's being complaining about tummyache for a while now, but today it was really bad,' Laura said. 'He rolled up into a ball with the pain and he was screaming. I didn't know what to do to help him. I just called for the ambulance straight away.'

'You did the right thing. I can see that he's very distressed. Do you want to stay with him and hold his hand?' Sarah was already beginning a preliminary examination.

'Yes, I do. I'm not leaving him.' She looked at Sarah, and there were tears in her eyes. 'Please, do what you can to help him.'

'I will. I'll take care of him, I promise. Is there anyone with you?'

'My husband's parents should be here any minute. They were with me when he was taken ill. I've been trying to get in touch with Harry. He's away from his office, but his line manager said he would contact him and get him to come over here as soon as possible.'

'All right. Try not to worry. If you stay calm it will help Nicky, I'm sure.' Sarah supposed that it was only to be expected that Matthew's parents would come along. They were bound to be anxious but, given the bad feeling between them and her family, she wasn't sure how she would cope if she came face to face with them.

Nicky was vomiting, and a nurse hurried to tenderly wipe his brow.

Sarah checked him over, being as gentle as she could. It was terribly upsetting to see this little boy looking so poorly. It was hard to believe that just a short time ago he had been with her and Matthew at the fair and the beach.

Now, as she examined him, she could see that his abdomen was distended, and she noted that he was also dehydrated and feverish. His pulse was rapid and his skin was pale, as though he was in a shocked state. She wished that Matthew was there. She would feel so much more confident in treating the child if he was by her side.

'We need to put in a nasogastric tube,' she told Helen, who was assisting, 'and we'll give him fluids. I can feel a mass in his abdomen, and that's worrying me. I think there some kind of obstruction in there, and from the looks of him we need to act quickly. I'm going to send him down to X-Ray so that we can find out what's going on.'

Turning to Laura, she explained, 'The X-ray should give us some idea of what's causing Nicky's discomfort. If you go with him it will help him to feel better about what's going on.'

They returned soon afterwards. 'What do the X-rays show?' Laura asked.

'It looks as though Nicky has what we call an intussusception,' Sarah told her. 'It's when part of the intestine folds back on itself, or telescopes, very much as if you pull a shirtsleeve inside itself.'

Laura frowned. 'What can you do about that?'

'We're going to give him a barium enema. That will help us to see more clearly what's going on in his intestine and the procedure itself might help to unfold that portion of the bowel.'

The child's mother nodded. 'I'm sure you know best. I just want to see him get better.'

Sarah and Helen worked together to try to clear the obstruction. After a while though, it was fairly obvious that the procedure wasn't working.

'What's happening?' Laura asked.

'Unfortunately,' Sarah said, 'we haven't been able to put things right. I think Nicky may need surgery, so I'm going to refer him right away. I'll get a nurse to talk to you and explain what's to happen. She'll give you some consent forms to sign.'

Laura was white-faced, but she nodded. 'I wanted to stay with him.'

'I know. It's only for a little while, and we'll take good care of him while you go through the paperwork. As soon as that's finished you can come back to him.'

Sarah stayed with Nicky a while longer, making sure that he was as comfortable as he could be. Then, after she had spoken to the surgeon, she left the nurse to prepare the child for Theatre and speak to Laura once again.

Laura was in the relatives' room, filling out the paperwork, and Sarah saw that Matthew's parents were there with her. She pulled in a deep breath and reminded herself that they were deeply unhappy about what had happened to their grandson. She would have to be sensitive in the way she handled them.

Matthew's mother looked shaken and distressed. 'I can't believe that he needs surgery,' she said. 'How can he go from being a lively, healthy little boy one minute to needing an operation the next? Are you sure that it's necessary?'

'I'm afraid it is, Teresa,' Sarah said. 'I've spoken with the surgeon, and he wants to operate straight away.'

'But you've already carried out one procedure on him,' Teresa objected, 'and that didn't work.' She pressed her hands together, her nails digging into her palms. 'I wish Matthew was here. Perhaps we could have avoided all this. He might have been able to do something so that Nicky didn't need an operation. He's our only grandson, and he's so tiny. I can't bear to think of him having to go through all that.'

Sarah bit her lip. Matthew's parents were obviously unhappy at having to deal with her, but there was nothing she could do about that. She wished that Matthew was here, too, if only because he might have backed her up. It was difficult at any time dealing with a child who was ill and in pain, and sometimes decisions had to be made very quickly. There was no time for hesitation, but it made her deeply uncomfortable to know that they didn't trust her to do the right thing.

'I'm afraid any delay would be very bad for Nicky,' Sarah said. 'There could be very serious consequences if he isn't treated immediately.'

Stephen hadn't said anything up to now, but his features were pale and Sarah could see that he was anxious. She turned to him and said quietly, 'I know that you would feel better if Matthew was treating Nicky, but I'm sure that he would have come to the same decision as I have.'

He grimaced. 'It's not that we doubt your ability,' he said. 'It's just that Matthew's very experienced. He's a consultant, and he might have seen children with this complaint many times before. He might have been able to come up with an alternative.'

'I haven't taken this decision on my own,' Sarah said, 'and if it helps at all, I have seen cases like Nicky's before this. The outcome is usually good provided that the problem is dealt with urgently.'

Laura intervened. 'I've already signed the papers,' she said. 'I trust Sarah to make the right decision, and I'm not going to delay and risk any setbacks with Nicky's condition.'

She handed the papers to Sarah. 'Go ahead and help him. Can I go with him to the theatre?'

'Yes, of course. You can be with him until his medication takes effect. I'll take you to him now, if you like.'

She led Laura back to A and E and supervised

Nicky's transfer to Theatre. All the time she was praying silently that everything would go well.

A short time later, she was startled to see Matthew enter the department. He was wearing an immaculate dark suit, but even as he came towards her he was shrugging out of the jacket.

'What are you doing here?' Sarah asked. 'I thought you were supposed be in Cornwall for the day.'

'My parents called me. I'd finished my talk and I managed to reschedule the question-and-answer session so that I could get away.' He frowned. 'They said they were worried that Nicky was to have surgery. Has that already begun?'

'I think it should be starting just about now,' she said. 'He looked so poorly. It was dreadful seeing him like that.' She hesitated. 'I think your parents believe I was wrong to send him for an operation.'

He frowned. 'Where are they?'

'They were in the relatives' room the last time I saw them. Your brother was on his way. I haven't had a chance to speak to him yet, but he might be glad if you could have a word with him.'

'I'll do that.'

He hurried away, and Sarah felt thoroughly despondent. She was glad he was back, but it bothered her that his parents had felt it necessary to contact him. They were unhappy at her decision to call for surgery and it was fairly obvious that they were hoping for a second opinion.

It was bad for Nicky that this had happened, but it had also brought about another downturn in the relationship between her family and Matthew's. There was a lot of history between her family and his, and lately not much of it was good.

It was some time before Matthew came back to her. 'Nicky's still in surgery,' he said. 'It's awful to think of him going through that.'

She nodded. 'The waiting seems unbearable, doesn't it? How are the rest of the family holding up?'

'Not too well. They're on edge and they're anxious about what might happen. As you say, the waiting is the worst time.' He glanced at her. 'Do you have time for a break?'

She nodded, and he walked with her to the doctors' lounge and pushed open the door.

'It's hard to imagine that Nicky is the same little boy who was so happy at the beach. He looked so ill when he was brought in.'

'Laura told me what happened. She was devastated.' He poured coffee for them both. 'I suppose no one can tell when something like this is going to happen.' He glanced at her. 'Your father goes for his operation soon, doesn't he?'

'Yes. It's scheduled for next week.'

'Let's hope that he feels better once it's done. He's had a lot to contend with lately.' His gaze narrowed on her. 'Did you tell him that Casey Morgan was here in the hospital?'

She shook her head. 'No, I didn't want to give him any reason to be anxious.'

'So he doesn't know that Robert is home and that he has been to see his father?'

'No. I decided he didn't need to know that.'

He pulled a face. 'That's a pity, because Rachel has been to see Robert, and he's persuaded her that he could help out while your father's in hospital. It might have been better if your father had been fore-warned about him turning up.'

Her eyes widened in shock. 'Why would Rachel do that?' She stared at him. 'This is your doing, isn't it? You persuaded Rachel that it would be a good idea for Robert to help out, yet you knew that I was against it. I don't want my dad upset. Don't you realise how that might affect him?'

'I think it could turn out to be for the good. Robert isn't a clone of his father. I think it was wrong that you didn't give him the chance to make amends. At least Rachel's open-minded and prepared to listen.'

She glared at him. 'What makes you so convinced that you know what's right? How can you assume that you know what's best for my family when you're not even doing right by Rachel and Emily?'

He sent her a quizzical look 'I've done what I can for them.'

'Have you? Then it isn't enough.'

'I'm not altogether sure that I know what you mean.'

'Don't you? Then perhaps I should spell it out for you. You and Rachel were a couple. Then you went away, and almost nine months later Rachel had a baby. Does that make things any clearer for you?'

His gaze was piercing. 'Am I getting this straight? Are you saying that you think I'm Emily's father?'

'That's exactly what I'm saying.'

His jaw tightened, a muscle clenching there. 'Then let me tell you here and now that you are wrong. I am *not* Emily's father, and I resent the fact that you could for one minute imagine that I would father a child and then casually abandon its mother. What kind of a man do you think I am?' He glared at her. 'You obviously don't know me at all.'

Sarah stared at him, open-mouthed. She was stunned by his reaction. She had never seen him so angry before, and it alarmed her that he could turn on her in such a way. His eyes were like flint, stabbing her as though he hated to even look at her.

'I don't even want to be in the same room as you.' He swung away from her and marched to the door. Then he went out, slamming it shut behind him.

Sarah's gaze was fixed on the door. Her legs felt weak and insubstantial all at once and she felt behind her for a chair. Sinking down into it, she let her mind run over what he had said.

It looked dreadfully as though she had made a terrible mistake, and at this moment she had absolutely no idea how she could put things right.

CHAPTER TEN

SARAH was stunned by what had just happened. How could she have got it so badly wrong?

For all this time she had believed that Matthew was Emily's father, and now he had denied it vehemently. She didn't know what to think any more. Had she really misjudged him all this time? Her mind was reeling in shock. The consequences of her mistake were too awful to contemplate.

She had alienated him by her accusation and, as if that wasn't bad enough, his family was against her, too.

The sound of an ambulance siren in the distance brought her back to the cold facts of everyday life. She had a job to do and she couldn't simply stand here feeling sorry for herself. There was work to be done, and as soon as she had the opportunity she would go and find out how Nicky was doing.

'Dr Carlisle…Sarah…' a man called after her as she walked along the corridor.

She looked up to see Robert Morgan hurrying towards her. Warily, she stopped.

He said awkwardly, 'I was hoping that I might see you again. I wanted to thank you for taking care of my father. I'm sure that he would have died if it hadn't been for you and what you did for him.'

'I'm sorry that I wasn't able to do more for him,' she said. 'He's still here in the hospital, isn't he?'

'Yes. I've just been up to see him.'

'He's stable for the moment, I believe.'

He nodded. 'He was well enough to talk to me.'

She frowned. 'I'm glad for you, but you know you shouldn't expect too much, don't you?'

'I realise that. I'm just glad for every extra day that he has—it gives me more of a chance to mend my relationship with him. We haven't been getting along very well for some years, but I've had time to think things through and I was afraid that he might die while things were still unsettled between us. You've given me a chance to put things right.'

He paused, watching her expression. 'Are you all right? I'm sorry, I've been going on about my concerns, but you look as though you have troubles of your own.'

She didn't answer. She had been mistaken about Matthew, and now she was wondering whether she had been wrong about Robert, too. He was doing his best to be friendly towards her, despite her earlier coolness towards him. Had she been so blinkered in her thinking that she ignored all the signs that came her way?

His brow furrowed. 'Or perhaps it's just that you don't want to talk to me. I know this must be difficult for you. My father treated you and your family very badly, but I hope you don't think that I'm the same as him. I know my father has a lot of faults. He's a weak man who took the easy way out, but I've never wanted to do that. For a long time I resented him for the way he made my mother's life miserable, and I vowed that I would be different.'

Sarah made an effort to pull herself together. She looked carefully at Robert and perhaps now she saw him properly for the first time. He looked earnest, as though he really meant what he was saying.

'I'm sorry for the way I treated you the other day, for the way I spoke to you,' she murmured. 'You're right, I was putting you on the same level as your father, and that was wrong of me. Perhaps I never got to know you very well.'

'I hope that we can start afresh. Is that possible?'

She nodded, still troubled by all that had happened. 'We can try.' She straightened, stiffening her spine. 'You'll have to excuse me now. I have to go and see to my patients.'

'Of course. I'm sorry for holding you up.'

She hurried away, anxious to get on with her work, and as soon as she had the chance she headed for the recovery room. She was sure that Nicky must have come out of Theatre by now, and she was anxious to find out how the surgery had gone.

'He had intussusception,' the surgeon told her. 'I've explained everything to the family. It was a good thing that you referred him to me as quickly as you did, because these things can be very nasty if they are not caught in time. As it is, he should be all right now. The surgery went well.'

She felt the tension drain out of her. 'Thank you. I'm relieved that you found the cause of the trouble.'

Sarah went back to A and E, consoling herself that at least Nicky was on the mend, even if everything else in her life was falling apart.

Matthew was working with a patient, and when he had finished she said to him hesitantly, 'I heard that Nicky has come through his surgery. Have you been to see him yet?'

He shook his head. 'No. I've been too busy here, but I'm going up there now.' He looked at her, his expression impassive. 'Were you thinking of coming with me?'

He didn't sound as though he wanted her to go with him, and she thought of all the barely suppressed hostility she had received from his parents when she had been trying to treat Nicky. It was probably not a good idea to show her face just now. The family would be upset and might resent her presence.

'I don't think so. There's nothing more I can do and I'm sure he's in good hands now.'

He nodded. 'If that's the way you want it.' His manner was icy towards her, and now he turned away as though she were a stranger to him. Feeling numb inside, she walked slowly away from him feeling as though she had just experienced a blast of Arctic winter.

Things didn't improve throughout the course of the day. He scarcely spoke to her unless it was absolutely necessary, and when she came to the end of her shift she went and collected her jacket and her bag and walked despondently out of the hospital.

She didn't see Matthew over the next couple of

days. She had some time off from work and she made the most of it, going to spend some time with her father, checking up on how he was feeling. His operation was imminent, and she and Rachel wanted to make sure that he was well enough to undergo the procedure.

'I'll be glad when it's all over,' he told them. 'It's been on my mind, and there are so many things I need to sort out before I go into hospital. Then there's the workshop…I have so many projects that I'm working on at the moment for clients and I can't afford to leave them. I still don't know what I'm going to do.'

'But you're not running a one-man business, are you?' Rachel said. 'You have men who work for you. Won't they be able to carry on while you're away?'

'To some extent they will, yes, but I need someone who has an overall vision, who can make managerial decisions. I don't have any one of that calibre. It's my fault. Ever since Casey let me down, I've not wanted to delegate responsibility. I thought I could manage.'

He made a brief smile. 'It's ironic, isn't it, that business is picking up just when I'm going to be out of action?'

Rachel said slowly, 'I thought you would say that. I wanted to talk to you about it, Dad. We've been trying to think of ways that we could help.' She glanced at Sarah, then back to her father and said, 'Sarah suggested that we get someone in who can get to grips with the work that you're doing. It could just be a temporary measure…someone from an agency, perhaps?'

Her father shook his head. 'It's a very specialised kind of work that we do in the workshop. It would take someone with real expertise to take over, and I just don't think it's going to happen.'

The doorbell rang, and Sarah went to answer it. Matthew was waiting there, and when she saw him her heart made a strange little flip-over. She felt relieved and comforted all at once, thoroughly glad to see him. He was dressed casually, wearing dark-coloured chinos and an open-necked shirt, and her skin warmed as she looked at him.

Her mouth made a faint curve. 'I wasn't expecting to see you,' she began, but he didn't return her smile, and she faltered.

'I came to see Rachel. She said she wanted to talk to me.'

'Oh…I see… Of course.' It hurt that he was so blunt and that his tone was so chill, but she tried to put a brave face on things. 'You had better come in.' She stood back and waved him into the hall. 'She's in the living room, talking to my dad.'

Her father wasn't in the room any longer, though, and Rachel said, 'He's gone out into the garden for a breath of air. His chest was troubling him again.'

She looked at Matthew and smiled. 'I'm glad you could come over. I feel so much better now that you're here. You always know what to do.'

He gave her a hug, and Sarah felt isolated, out in

the cold. 'You're worried about your father, aren't you?' he said.

'Yes. I'm still not sure how to put it to him—this business of asking Robert to help out.'

She sent Sarah a guilty glance. 'I meant to talk to you about it, Sarah, but I was always nervous about bringing the subject up.'

'I'm sorry.' Sarah's mouth moved awkwardly. 'It worries me that you feel there are things you can't talk to me about. It shouldn't be that way between us.' She hesitated. 'I don't understand how you think Robert can help. What can he do?'

'Perhaps you don't remember that he used to work with Dad in the business, before all the trouble flared,' Rachel said. 'You were away at medical school for some of the time. Robert was there to learn, and he was trying to work his way up the ladder, but then everything fell apart and he felt obliged to leave.'

She ran hand nervously through her hair. 'Since then, he's tried really hard to get the best qualifications that he can. These last few years he's been concentrating on getting his degree and specialising in the kind of work that Dad does. He's always been interested in design engineering, and ever since his mother was taken ill with asthma, he's wanted to do something on the medical side to improve patients' well-being. He's done wonderfully well. When you talk to him you just know that he's going to be exactly the right person to work with Dad.'

Sarah studied Rachel curiously. When she was talking about Robert, she was more animated than she had been in a long time. Her eyes glowed with pride, and there was a softness about her features.

Light dawned on Sarah in a sudden sunburst of realisation. She said slowly, 'You're in love with him, aren't you?'

Rachel gave her a wary look, and then slowly nodded. 'I think I've always loved him, almost from the moment I first saw him.'

'Why didn't you ever tell me? Why did you keep me in the dark about what was going on for so long?'

'How could I tell you? After what his father did, after the way he ruined Dad's business, I felt as though we were doomed. Dad would never have had him in the house, and you had been stung as much as any of us. You used all your savings to see Dad through that awful time. How could I tell either of you that I was in love with Robert? I would have felt like a traitor if I'd gone on seeing him. Anyway, he went away. He thought it was for the best. That way, he wouldn't cause any upheaval for us.' She winced. 'He didn't know about Emily, and I never told him.'

So Robert was Emily's father. Sarah felt terrible. She went and put her arms around her sister and held her close. 'I'm so sorry. You've had to bear this all on your own. I wish things had been different...I wish you could have felt able to tell me. I might have understood.'

Rachel shook her head. 'It wouldn't have worked out. You might have let something slip to Dad, and then his health might have suffered even more. It's been bad enough as it is. I've been worried that the slightest thing would give him a heart attack.' She grimaced, straightening up, and Sarah let her go, watching her cautiously. 'Even now, I don't know how I'm going to tell him the truth. I don't want to do anything to push him over the edge.'

Matthew said briskly, 'Don't you think it's time that you started to live your own life, Rachel? You can't keep on worrying endlessly about your father. Over the last few months he's come to realise that Morgan has lost everything…his marriage has fallen apart, he's lost the respect of his son and his health is failing. Your father isn't blind and he can see all this for himself. I believe he's come to terms with that, and I'm sure that you'll find the right words to tell him how you feel about Robert. Just tell him how hard he's worked to make something of himself, and how much he wants to try to make amends for the past.'

'I can't tell him. How can I do that?' Rachel looked at him in despair. 'What if it makes him ill again? He needs to be strong for the operation.'

He put his hands gently on her shoulders and turned her around. 'Right now he's more worried about how the business is going to fare while he's in hospital, and the stress is doing him no good at all. You need to go and tell him the truth and stop worrying about the consequences. Sarah and I are both here to look after him if anything should happen. When it all finally sinks in, he'll probably feel a lot better about his stay in hospital and the aftermath. A lot of niggling questions will have been answered and, who knows, he may even feel reassured to have Robert take charge.'

Rachel bit her lip. 'If you're sure…?' She still looked doubtful.

Sarah said quickly, 'Do you want me to come with you?'

Rachel shook her head. 'No, I'll do this on my own. I need to take it slowly, to think about what I'm going to say.'

'All right, then. Good luck.'

'Thanks, Sarah.' Rachel sent her a shaky smile. She paused, and then added, 'I hadn't expected you to take all of this so well.'

Sarah made a face. 'I've learnt a lot these last few weeks. I'm just beginning to come to terms with all of it. I've made such a mess of things. You felt you couldn't confide in me, and I'm terribly ashamed about that.'

'It wasn't your fault…you mustn't think that. It was my concern for Dad that made me hesitate, not you.'

Straightening her shoulders, Rachel went out to the garden, leaving Sarah alone with Matthew.

Sarah pulled in a deep breath. 'I was wrong about you and Rachel,' she murmured, 'and I'm sorry for the things I said to you. I had no idea about Robert and she hadn't given me even a hint of what was going on. I wish I had known. I thought you and she were a couple.'

'Rachel and I have always been friends,' he murmured. 'It was probably only natural that it would turn out that way. My family and yours lived close to each other for so many years that she and I were almost like brother and sister. We got on well together, and everything else developed from that.'

'I can see that now. I think it was when you went to live together that I started to get the idea there was something more.'

'It was expedient to share a flat. We were both studying, and it helped that we shared the cost. With others in the flat as well, I don't think it occurred to either of us that people would draw the wrong conclusion.'

Sarah winced. 'Rachel always drew admirers, but she didn't appear to have eyes for any of them except you. Did you know about Robert?'

'Yes, I guessed that there was something going on. You were away at medical school most of the time, so perhaps that's why you didn't see it. I was closer to her and I put two and two together. They kept it quiet, probably because they were unsure of themselves to begin with and afterwards because of what his father did.'

Distressed, she looked up at him. 'Why didn't you tell me? All this time I knew nothing about what had been going on.'

He gave a light shrug. 'She asked me not to tell anyone. She was afraid the slightest hint would mean that your father would get to know. He hasn't been well for a long time and that coloured everything she did.'

'Didn't you realise that I had the wrong idea about you?'

He looked into her eyes, and his expression was unreadable. 'I hoped you would remember that you and I had been friends for a long time. I thought that you knew me and understood me, and that you would believe in my integrity.' A muscle flicked in his jaw. 'I was wrong.'

Sarah felt as though she had been dealt a blow. How could she have been so badly wrong? Would he ever forgive her?

He didn't say any more, and at that moment Rachel and her father walked in through the patio doors. Her father looked white and shaken.

Matthew and Sarah helped him into a chair.

When he was a little more composed, her father glanced up at Matthew. 'Rachel has just been telling me about Robert. I don't know what to think any more. All this time I thought that you were... Well, obviously I was wrong.' He broke off, frowning, a little embarrassed.

Matthew pulled a face. 'Don't feel too badly about it. You're not the only one, it seems.' He glanced briefly at Sarah, his lips making a straight line, and then he returned his gaze to her father. 'Have you decided what you're going to do?'

'I don't know. Rachel suggested that I let Robert take over while I'm away, but I'm not at all sure about that. I don't want to make the same mistake again. How do I know that I can trust him?'

'You won't, unless you give him the chance. The only way round it might be to draw up a legal agree-

ment and get him to sign it. I could act as his guar-
antor, if you like.'

Her father was surprised. 'Would you be prepared
to do that?'

Matthew nodded. 'I've been getting to know him
better recently. He isn't like his father. He felt bad
about the way his mother was let down, and he moved
away with her so that he could take care of her for
these last few years. He's worked hard and he wants
to prove himself, to make up for everything that's
gone wrong. His father was a skilled engineer, but he
let his talents go to waste. He thought drink would
solve his problems, but in the end it was his undoing.'

His mouth made a slight curve. 'Robert is completely different. He's strong and he's determined,
and he's also highly skilled. I think he deserves a
chance.'

Sarah looked anxiously at her father. He was still
frowning, but at least there was more colour in his
cheeks now, and she felt that the danger of a crisis
might have passed.

'Perhaps,if I let him work with me for a short time,
I'll be able to come to a decision,' her father ventured.
'There's still a little time before my operation. It
might just give me long enough to make up my mind
about him.'

Rachel gave a soft sigh of relief. She went over to
him and hugged him. 'Thank you for that. I know it
will all work out in the end. He won't let you down,
you'll see.'

Matthew's bleeper sounded, and he checked it

briefly, and then said, 'I have to go. I'm needed at the hospital.' He glanced at her father. 'I think you've made the right decision. I'll talk to you again later.'

Sarah didn't want him to go. She desperately needed to talk to him, but he moved swiftly towards the door and went out to his car without acknowledging her. He switched on the engine and a few seconds later all she could see was his car in the distance.

He wasn't at work when she went back on duty. 'He's involved in management meetings,' Helen told her, 'and then he has some teaching commitments. They've brought in a locum consultant to take his place for the next couple of weeks.'

Sarah felt empty inside. She was lost without him, and for the first time she realised how much she missed him when he wasn't there. It was as though the world was suddenly a darker place.

On the day of her father's operation, she made sure that she was at his bedside. He was calm, ready for what was about to happen, and it seemed that he was the one who was reassuring her.

'I'll be fine,' he said, squeezing her hand. 'I feel a lot better now that I know things are working out with the business. Matthew was right. Robert's a good man. He has a good grasp of management and he can troubleshoot situations that would throw another man off course. I think things will be safe in his hands.'

'You shouldn't be thinking about any of that right now,' Sarah chided him gently. 'Just concentrate on getting yourself better.'

She was nervous about the procedure he was to

undergo. What if something went wrong? As a doctor, she knew all the pros and cons, but this was her father and it was impossible for her to be relaxed about the situation. It was as much she could do to keep her fears from him.

A nurse came to usher her away. 'It's almost time for him to go up to Theatre,' she said lightly. 'Do you want to say goodbye to him now, and then come back this afternoon?'

Sarah leaned over and tenderly kissed her father's cheek. 'I won't be far away,' she told him.

Rachel said her goodbyes, and watched as the nurse wheeled him away. She pulled in a deep breath, then turned to Sarah. 'I have to go and fetch Emily from nursery school,' she said. 'I'll be back in time to see him on the ward. Will you be all right?'

Sarah nodded. 'Yes, of course. You go.'

'Where will you be?'

'I haven't thought about it. I suppose I'll go for a walk. Perhaps I'll head for the park. It's near enough for them to contact me if I'm needed. I have asked the nurse to let me know as soon as there's any news.'

She went there. She often walked in the park when she needed peace and quiet. Her favourite place was by the lakeside, where she could watch the ducks glide along the water or sun themselves on the grassy bank.

She stood still and watched them now, and absorbed herself in the reflections on the shimmering surface of the lake.

'Rachel told me that I would find you here.' The

familiar deep voice sounded in her ear, and she was suddenly filled with happiness.

She turned to look at him. 'Matthew,' she said softly, a smile tentatively touching her lips. 'I thought you were away this week. Helen said that you were teaching.'

'I managed to get away. I knew this was the day your father was coming into hospital, and I thought you might need some support.'

'You were right. I was feeling sorry for myself, but now I'm so glad that you're here. I've missed you.' Her smile wavered. 'It's selfish of me, isn't it, thinking of myself at a time like this? I'm so desperately worried about him. He's always been there for us and I can't bear to think of anything happening to him.'

Matthew put an arm around her. 'I'm here now. You're not alone.' He turned her to face him. 'Besides, nothing's going to happen to him. He'll come through this and be much stronger. You have to believe that.'

'I know, and I'm sure you're right. I don't know what's the matter with me, but I keep thinking of everything that can go wrong.' She looked up at him. 'Thank you for coming here. I've never felt so alone in my life, and you're the only one who can make me feel better. You don't know how much it means to me to have you here. I thought you hated me and it made me feel awful.'

He gave her a rueful smile. 'I could never hate you. I wanted to be with you. I knew how unhappy you would be, and I wanted to be here for you, to take care of you.' He looked down at her, and his finger traced the line of her cheek. 'It's all I've ever wanted.'

Her eyes widened. 'Is it?'

'Oh, yes. Don't you know how much I care for you?'

Her gaze was uncertain. 'Do you? Care for me, I mean.'

'More than anything. I love you, Sarah. I've always loved you.'

She stared at him, and suddenly her eyes blurred with the sheen of tears. 'Can it really be true?'

'It's true.' His mouth gave a faint smile. 'For years now I've known that you were the only woman I could ever love. You're perfect. You're everything I've ever wanted in a woman. You're beautiful, you're spirited, caring and considerate. Why would I ever look at anyone else?'

Her eyes widened. 'But you never said anything to me about how you felt. I didn't know. How could I know?'

He smoothed his hands down her spine as though he would calm her. 'I couldn't say anything. You were so young, and you were going away to medical school. You were just setting out in life, and there was so much you had still to experience. I couldn't hold you back. It would have been wrong to do that.'

'You wouldn't have been holding me back. You would have made me so happy. Don't you know that?' She lifted her hand and touched his face. 'I wanted you to love me. I've loved you for ever, but you always seemed to keep a distance between us, and I couldn't understand what I had done wrong.'

He bent his head towards her and kissed her tenderly on the lips. 'You hadn't done anything wrong at all. I daren't show you how much I cared for you. It would have ruined everything. You might never have gone away and done all those things that you needed to do. I would have held you back, and in the end you might have come to blame me for that. You would have felt restless, and yearned for all the things you never had.'

She shook her head. 'No. I wanted you. No one else. Nothing else. And all the time I believed that you were in love with Rachel, and I felt so guilty for loving you.'

He kissed her again, and this time there was a hunger in him, as though he could never get enough of her, or she of him. She wanted the kiss to go on and on for ever.

'We've wasted so much time,' he said raggedly, coming up for air. 'We can't waste any more.' His hands cupped her shoulders, drawing her even closer to him. 'Say that you'll marry me, that you'll be my wife. I need to know that you'll be by my side for ever, that I won't ever have to spend another day without you.'

She looked up at him and there was uncertainty in her gaze. 'I want to, more than anything in the world. I want to say yes, but it won't work, will it? There are your parents to consider. They don't like me. They didn't want me to treat Nicky, and they're still at odds with my father. How can we be together when they feel that way? In the end, aren't they just another barrier to keep us apart?'

He shook his head. 'Is that why you wouldn't come and see Nicky? Because you thought they wouldn't want you there?'

'I didn't want to be the cause of any more bad feeling. It was a bad time for them, and I thought me being there would make it worse.'

'It wasn't like that. I spoke to them and told them that you had done the right thing when you treated Nicky, and the surgeon only emphasised what I had said. They were upset when Nicky was taken ill, and they weren't thinking logically. They thought Nicky needed someone with a lot more experience to take care of him, but they realised afterwards that you had done everything possible for him, and that you had probably saved his life by acting so quickly. They were disappointed when you didn't come to see him after the surgery, because they wanted to tell you how grateful they were. They looked for you later, but you had already left the hospital.'

'I remember that I was upset. You had seemed so cool towards me, and I didn't know what to do to put things right.'

'I just needed time so that I could come to terms with everything. I was disappointed that you hadn't believed in me, and that you hadn't trusted me to do the right thing. I would never abandon my own child.'

He drew her to him and brushed her forehead with his lips. 'It took me a while to realise how it must have been for you. You had looked out for Rachel and your father for so many years without a thought for yourself, and you were doing it even then. You were worried about Rachel, and you saw things from her point of view. I knew that somehow I had to explain things to you, but I had promised Rachel that I would keep quiet.'

'She must have changed her mind about that. Was it just Robert coming back that made her think differently?'

'No. It was more than that. I told her that we couldn't go on this way any longer. It was time that you knew the truth, and I wasn't prepared to leave you in the dark any longer. I said that I would be there to help her if she needed me.'

'Do you think she and Robert will get together?'

He smiled. 'I don't think there's anything that will keep them apart now.' His expression sobered. 'I'm more concerned about you and me. Do we have a future together?'

She lifted her hands to his face and placed a kiss on his lips. 'Oh yes…yes. I love you, and I want to be with you for always.'

His arms closed around her, and he sealed their love with a kiss that was as warm as the summer sun and as perfect as the hot blue sky overhead.

They only surfaced when Sarah heard the soft ring tones of her mobile. She checked the caller's number and looked up at him in dismay. 'It must be the hospital,' she said worriedly. 'Surely it's too soon? They can't have finished the procedure yet, can they?'

He glanced at his watch. 'It's possible,' he said. 'Answer it and find out.'

His arm was firm and steady around her waist as he waited for her to finish her conversation with the nurse. 'Well, what do they say?' he asked when she finally cut the call.

'He's all right,' she said, her mouth curving in a smile. 'The procedure went more smoothly than they could have hoped for, and now he's resting. They say I should be able to go and see him in about an hour.'

She paused. 'Apparently, your parents have been asking after him. They want to know if it would be all right for them to visit, and the nurse said that she would check with me first.'

'I told you that he would be all right, didn't I?' He hugged her long and hard and then said, 'What will you do about my parents?'

'I said that we would tell him first and prepare him. I don't see any reason why it would upset him to see them if they are only concerned about his well-being. Did you tell them that he was going into hospital?'

He nodded. 'I've tried to keep them up to date with what was happening. I thought it might help to reconcile them with him. Too many things have gone wrong over the last few years, and it's time that they were put right.'

'I'm going to go to the hospital now to see him,' she said. 'Will you come with me?'

'Of course I will. That's why I'm here...to help you and be by your side. Besides, I think we should be together when we tell him our good news, don't you?'

His mouth curved in a smile. 'Do you think he'll be well enough for a late summer wedding?'

She gave that some thought. 'How long does that give us? A few weeks?'

He nodded. 'That's what I had in mind.'

'That's plenty of time, I should think. With lots of tender loving care, we'll soon have him back on his feet.'

'Just one more thing before we go…'

She lifted her gaze to him. 'Yes…what is it?'

'I need to hold you, to be sure that I'm not imagining this.'

She went into his arms, and they held each other tight, and this time, when they kissed, it was a promise of all the joy that was still to come.

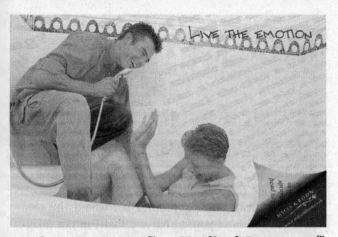

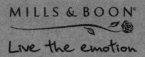

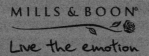

FREE

4 BOOKS
AND A SURPRISE GIFT!

We would like to take this opportunity to thank you for reading this Mills & Boon® book by offering you the chance to take FOUR more specially selected titles from the Medical Romance™ series absolutely FREE! We're also making this offer to introduce you to the benefits of the Reader Service™——

- ★ FREE home delivery
- ★ FREE monthly Newsletter
- ★ FREE gifts and competitions
- ★ Exclusive Reader Service discount
- ★ Books available before they're in the shops

Accepting these FREE books and gift places you under no obligation to buy; you may cancel at any time, even after receiving your free shipment. Simply complete your details below and return the entire page to the address below. *You don't even need a stamp!*

YES! Please send me 4 free Medical Romance books and a surprise gift. I understand that unless you hear from me, I will receive 6 superb new titles every month for just £2.69 each, postage and packing free. I am under no obligation to purchase any books and may cancel my subscription at any time. The free books and gift will be mine to keep in any case.

M4ZEF

Ms/Mrs/Miss/Mr ....Initials ....
BLOCK CAPITALS PLEASE

Surname ....

Address ....

....

....Postcode ....

Send this whole page to:
UK: FREEPOST CN81, Croydon, CR9 3WZ
EIRE: PO Box 4546, Kilcock, County Kildare (stamp required)